THE NEW BIZARRO AUTHOR SERIES
PRESENTS

EVISCERATOR

FARAH ROSE SMITH

ERASERHEAD PRESS
PORTLAND, OREGON

ERASERHEAD PRESS
P.O. BOX 10065
PORTLAND, OR 97296

www.eraserheadpress.com
facebook/eraserheadpress

ISBN: 978-1-62105-258-6
Copyright © 2018 by Farah Rose Smith
Cover design copyright © 2018 Eraserhead Press

Printed in the USA.

Editor's Note

Farah Rose Smith's Eviscerator is a sad, Dark Wave head trip, like a Siouxsie and the Banshees song given malevolent life by Derek Jarman. In a world where mad science meets New Wave, without the comforts of Devo and Thomas Dolby, we meet Gut Ghouls, toilet worms and a sexy punk super scientist who Benton Quest and Reed Richards would drool over at the club but never truly understand. This year has more experiments in form than I've fielded in previous years and I think the genre will be enriched by that. Eviscerator is weird in so many ways and exciting in so many others. Is the whimper of Eliot's Hollow Men the plaintive wail of Robert Smith? Spike up your hair and leave all hope behind.

—Garrett Cook, editor

For the sick girls

I cannot eat, but breathe
I cannot drink, but dry up.
I cannot love, but lie alone in hunger.

I touch my tongue to the dust of the earth and think myself sated; in this way, I am fooled by no one but myself.

I want no more inside. Having more is to accept poison as pleasure. And yet, enough is not enough. The body grows more feeble.

I will not know taste as pleasure. There is always the fear of death by mouth. They will say it is by choice and choice-derangement, and for many, this may be true. I have not known taste without torment since meeting the Eviscerator. It is my predicament—the gut as hall of dismay. There is no loathing of the body rooted so deeply as that of hunger. What it does to the mind—so unremitting in its devastation, that one without fuel can be nothing but alien in the elevated world. Thoughts will allow nothing more.

How am I to ever explain this to anyone? To live? They don't know the horrors of eternal poison, that that which nourishes them suffocates me. And for them to know and

7

care is a dream. Such things are the precursors to endless solitude, aloneliness that births a t starvation of its own.

I speak because speaking is the only feast afforded. I may spit and writhe—an agony of words that can't be silenced by the gut—in the street, on stage. Only by the mind that knows a starving tongue is not at home in this festive world. I waste away, and I worry. I die the slowest death afforded by time. I am still afraid. Always afraid.

I cannot eat, but breathe
I cannot drink, but dry up.
I cannot love, but lie alone in hunger.

The autumn landscape screams hideousness. Currents of warm air and grey light curse the city. Enormous, twisting, shimmering, jagged spirals of metal shoot out of the ground, horror in situ. Transfixed and unable to decipher the meaning of the artless things, Vex Valis succumbs to the divination of open spaces. The bird of tears sits on the rubbish heap, cruelly frail, marking the procession with meaningless meaning. A bloodbath, oil, and breath.

Her boot is on his throat. Snorts pull up that heavy plastic smell, caked in the dirt and grime of the back alley night spot where they all go to forget. Discount vinyl in emerald green, and a heel that could carve a half-moon into his forehead with the slightest twist of her ankle. She's being merciful today.

"I don't remember the word!"

Pressure bears down on him. Vex pushes her other heel into his wrist. He winces as she leans her face over his.

"I know, Charlie."

The weight of her limbs retracts. Charlie shoots up and runs several paces to his clothes. Vex sits down on the bed, swinging his keys on her index finger. He watches them swing back and forth before reaching out to grab them. She allows it. The man scrambles out the door, not bothering to close it behind him.

If you play, you play with the dead.

He forgot his briefcase. She pops it open, eyes falling immediately onto a pack of unopened gummi bears in the upper right corner with a tiny note that says *Lucy*.

"Another daddy."

She tears open the pack and pours them past her lips. Chewing slowly, savoring the chemical sugar shit. It's been four years since she put food in her mouth. Long enough for her to almost forget what comes next. Bloody phlegm pours out of her mouth and nose. Blinded by burning tears that sting her face, she scrapes her plastic nails on her knees to transfer the pain. More blood. More vomit. She shouldn't have eaten them. She can't eat again.

Darkness. Dark-ness. Still. No motion. Sickness. Vex Valis. My girl.

What happened to Vex was so rare that she felt herself in the presence of a celestial scheme in motion at all times. Many complaints were leveled against her, but to heed them was to coddle mortality. Youth was a force, age was the grave. One would think that greater worlds had found a way to live far beyond their natural allowance, but left to her own devices, she could laugh at such assumptions, once. She did as countless others did. Their subconscious minds were open wounds, endlessly scraped by every injustice mounted onto the public platform. She had no time for such things. For years, Vex walked through the earth with a singular mind, until the gut ghouls began chewing. Friends spoke to her of nature. Of animals. Of instinctual inevitability and reptilian brains. She looks in mirrors and sees only herself. Should have listened to the voices? Not merely advocates of flesh and fancy? She can't fathom how, in such a condition, she lives. A machine with skin; a monstrosity, they tell her.

Vex Valis.

Some days she walks through a crowd and wants to fuck everybody. Some days she walks through and wants to kill everybody. And sometimes she just walks.

Terror overtakes her. Paralyzed momentarily, she forces herself to pick up her head. She closes her eyes tightly, attempting to wipe the violent memories from her mind. Attempting to bury them is overwhelming. She wonders if she died in the arms of the Eviscerator and entered some kind of beggar's limbo, but suspects that is not the case. There is something strangely foreign in the air. Even when she breathes, she inhales a creeping repulsion. Too serious. Too wretched. Too *sick*. Her mind is an open sore, unable to filter out information in any way which would make day to day life bearable, let alone worth living.

But she lives.

Vex is on the floor of the bathroom in the Black Parlour Club; scraped knees under ripped nylon stockings. Deep-V vinyl, vermilion locks falling to her waist, a stiff bundle at the crown of her head, sprayed and spiked into oblivion. She hears the sound of a tiny trumpet and lifts her head.

'Have you been to Wonderland?" Sticking out of the toilet, an administrative worm stares as she picks herself up from the filth. She knows he means the sewer.

"Not lately."

"Gut ghouls?"

Vex rubs her stomach, running her fingers over the deep black scar on her torso. The skin raises up in traveling lumps and retracts.

"Still hungry."

Stomach specters. It's the ghouls that make the

mayhem. They sip and suck at interior flesh. Little demons nourishing on the body and mind. If she eats, they turn inward and suck on the soul. Yet another reason to starve.

"Hmm?!??!"

The worm spits white pus onto her face. She closes her eyes, wiping it off in disgust, though unable to purge the drops that dissolved on her tongue.

"I have a show to finish, you fuck!"

"Heh! Heh heh!"

The worm disappears down the toilet before she has time to grab him. Vex slams the lid down as roars from the outside crowd grow louder. Plucked from the grey infirmity. Orange clouds. Purple plasma. The smell of cinnamon, turpentine, sulfur, and roses. Birthed from the frail obscurity. With what feels like thousand-year eyes opening for the first time, she watches her surroundings with delicate precaution, ebbing in and out of dream-delirium. A voice grows in her head, whispering to her…

As she struggles to remain conscious, living-dead doll Ana Cristalen—white-haired, ice-eyes circled in charcoal dust, sequins-and-fur-pandemonium—walks in and stares at her through the mirror.

"Hungry, bitch?"

Vex washes her hands in silence. She turns around to face the woman, grotesquely opulent and snide.

"Starving."

"Oh? Then why the mid-song departure?"

Ana Cristalen moves towards the mirror, removing a leather pouch from her coat, unzipping it, pulling out a long black tube of moldy lipstick.

Vex sneers at her and leaves.

The Black Parlour is full. Patrons scream, indecipherable sounds of lust and longing. Vex returns to the stage, licking the last of worm-juice off of her fingers and grabbing the microphone. Strangely satiated, the rarest feeling, she starts to scream.

"ECSTASY OF THE VOID."

The crowd returns her call, distortion pours in. The show has begun.

Strange mushrooms grew near the fallen stones around the property. Faintly lavender or blue, twisting and turning in the unlikeliest of fashions. Ana tried to imagine what kind of faeries might sit on such things but she then remembered a tale that forbade faeries from sitting on the mushrooms in the presence of aging spirits. It informed the moment. She wasn't a believer in much in those times.

It was the portraits that brought her to the outskirts of France. Though housed in Dr. Bailey's Hexes and Histories Museum in the United States before its condemnation, the whereabouts of the portraits had been a mystery for over a decade. Rumor brought her overseas, after several inquiries and countless months led to a long-sought correspondence with Dr. Brague Collins. A modern-day mad genius in his own right. Collins was a man of both profound intellect and controversy. Newly confiscated purchase records had shown that he was the present owner of the Desecration Portraits, horrid works by the German artist, Goethern Ellis Von Aurovitch. Ana Cristalen, in her graduate research phase, had been sent to bring him back to the

States with the series. How willfully one accepts a task that is far beyond their grasp when young.

She'd heard very little of Dr. Collins in the previous years. The lawsuit that initiated his self-induced European exile had occurred long before she was of age to understand it. Only when Ana began delving into case studies in her medical journalism course did she become acquainted with the details of his experiments. Unethical, barbaric, insidious, deranged. Many assigned a character to the man who was once the most prolific figure in medical research and disease eradication. Ana had my doubts as to the legitimacy of the accusations, but in those times she adhered to a kind of moral absolutism that is only truly seen in elaborate fiction.

He asked if they could meet at a small, decrepit chateau to avoid the onslaught of media outlets hunting for him. She agreed, looking forward to a bit of a hike in the sharp wind. One with wisdom seldom passes up a walk in the natural world. Although her haste and immaturity blinded her to the realities of wandering alone on a distant road. Thankfully she arrived unscathed to find the man himself sitting at a small, rickety wicker table outside of the structure. He was recognizable only by demeanor; in a haze of calamity. He had aged tremendously from the last time he appeared on television. That had been a few weeks before the death of his wife, Marcella.

Collins stood upon approach and introduced himself, despite being startled by what she could only assume was her youth. It seemed as though he thought they had met before. The inevitable exchange of trivialities began. She watched his eyes for signs of madness, but found none. He was a far less formidable figure than he had been purported to be. She saw no reason to hesitate with her reason for being there.

"Have you been watching the news?" She asked, as he pulled her chair out for her.

"I'm out of range, thankfully, for most technology, by design." He poured her a glass of tea in a delicate yellow cup that seemed to change shape upon contact with the heat.

"Then you are unaware of the new affliction?"

His eyes, curiously wide, grew cold.

"I am aware."

"And of its breadth? Its scope and impact?"

"I am aware," he replied again, examining her face closely. Unnerved by his gaze, Ana averted her eyes to the cup and continued.

"Dr. , I'm here to ascertain the whereabouts of the Desecration Portraits of Von Aurovitch."

He lowered his eyes and smiled slightly, leaning back in his chair.

"What do you know of Von Aurovitch?"

"I'm acquainted with his work. Vaguely."

"Then you best leave it there."

She raised her head again.

"Who did you sell the Desecration portraits to?"

"They weren't sold."

"Were they destroyed?"

"No."

"Dr."

He admires her vigor, her insistence.

"The Desecration Portraits have returned to Tharingia."

"In private ownership? In collection?"

"They have returned to the place of their birth, and like the grotesquery they depict, they will be burned."

"That can't happen. Dr. Collins, I was sent here to issue a full pardon to you for your offenses. Your abilities are still highly regarded in the States and we would like you to return and find the cure to this awful thing. But we need your cooperation, and we need the portraits."

Collins hesitated.

"How do you know of the portraits?" he asked her.

"They are the only known media that accurately depict..."

"Spontanabre."

Ana dropped the cup, shattering it on the marble table.

IN URGENCY: VEX VALIS

This notice comes to you on the present day, 17 AUGUST, 2019. To notify you of the following: You have DISOBEYED the EVISCERATOR in your continual noncompliance regarding his INSTRUCTIONS pertaining to the PROCUREMENT of the identity of the CONSPIRATOR in the TRANSPORTAL WORD. Be advised that you are scheduled for a VISITATION and will be notified SHORTLY as to the location and time.

Regards,
Q. T. MALIC
ORDER OF THE EVISCERAL SECRATERIUM

She remembers the Eviscerator. The voyages into the sheath. The death of Aaron. How she laughed at her own mutilation, touched herself to his telepathic tones. She remembers.

There are places beyond the gates of the stratosphere where stolen voices call out. Vex hopes she'll never hear them again. New diseases pop up like weeds. Every day, there seems to be a progression of some virus, some plague. She knows enough to not be afraid.

"So what if he needs the Conspirator? You'll find them and tell him."

Arthur rolls his head back onto the moldy couch, sandy hair grazing ripped leather. He no longer tries to control the guttural twitches. They send his limbs up like the wooden appendages of a marionette. Hearty tugs on sightless strings. Vex kicks the TV over.

"Don't take it out on my shit, kid."

"Don't you know there's only a few of us left?"

"What about Ana?"

Vex snorts.

"What about her?"

Vex sits down next to him on the couch, hitting the cushions with a hard thump.

"I bet it's her."

Arthur's right arm begins to twitch violently. Vex runs her hand slowly down his arm until it rests over his. The twitch slows.

"Have you ever thought, or allowed yourself to think, that maybe this is all bullshit? That there is no Conspirator, and it's just a game he's playing?"

Vex leans her head back, breathing slowly. She doesn't answer for some time.

"I've considered it."

"Then why don't you consider doing to him exactly what he did to you and me?"

She thinks quietly for a moment.

"Oh, I have."

"He's having a good laugh at us, isn't he?"

"And a good meal, to boot."

A sharp pang cuts through her stomach. She hasn't put much thought into what the Eviscerator must have done with their organs. Not from lack of imagination, but from the inability to reconcile such horrors in her head. She was a mess of self-implanted plastic tubing, adopted cartilage, and gut ghouls. Starving, eternally. Forced into submission.

"He ripped my guts out, too. Don't forget."

"I remember."

"Ok. Because it's not just a "vengeance for Vex" thing. I don't even have any fucking legs."

The toaster oven shuts off.

"You still get the sickness?"

"Every fucking time. Yeah. I make them for the smell."

"That's a good adaptation."

"Something like that."

Hunger knows no chaos like the intercourse of nose and nourishment. The amps cranked to maximum, that static sanctuary—that's her only sustenance. Music is her only food.

"I have a show tonight." She stands, adjusting her ripped stockings to show her bug tattoos.

"Are up for it?" Arthur asks, reaching out for her hand.

"I have to be."

It would be simple to say that I had imagined myself normal in the confines of my oppression. That I'd rarely been graced by the horrors of my condition as they had manifested in the outside world. When exposed to rats, and airs, and men alike. I imagined myself a perfectly preserved specimen in such a confinement. Though perhaps not perfect in the absolute sense. Perfect in my mess-protected in it. There is something of a glamour to being fractured and sheltered at once. To find some quiet justice in oneself that leads to isolation. Most would shame such a thing. Their tongues would wag in speeches of laziness and worthlessness, spittle aiming towards me—towards me, accusatory, without consideration that to be, as they have been, I would have to have been born as they were born.

The gala was a gathering of entrenched pretension found so often in places where humility should reign. When Dr. Valis' work finally came around to the social sphere, a research benefit had been arranged to honor the preliminary—and to date, only—discoveries and tragedies of the Transpermia Project. Vex knew women who would revel at the thought of standing on that stage. The glory, the honor. And that is not to say that she didn't deserve it on the merits of her work. But of her character, there was that lurking question. Where others beckoned Dr. Valis to help them in their crippling hour, she turned a blind eye. She suffered on a stage with smiles and laughs and crueler intentions than theirs. That is the odor of success. They called her the lion's darling, and she wore that title with quiet dishonor for a time.

She allowed Aaron that night of *honor*, knowing that while she stood there, he sat at home, confined to his wheelchair. It was that night that Vex first allowed her conscious mind to assign, quite accurately, responsibility for the containment failure to Dr. Cristalen. She was that kind of detestable genius who, despite her gifts of intellect and imagination, could not conceive of the possibility that anyone else might carry that potential. That is, perhaps, the curse of our leaders. It would take far more than trivial dismissals to charge her annoyance into fury. She had always known, somewhere, what she was capable of. Between her ego and her strange correspondence with Dr. Collins after grad school. Vex buried it. Most likely in the aftermath of Aaron's affliction, her capacity to measure morality became limited. If that was the case, the barrier was breaking.

The stage lights were blinding. Ana's speech was drowned out by applause and the mind's wanderings. Between the rays of light, Vex could see only her teeth. The night went by quickly after she allowed her senses to wander. The dread of the evening could never be as great as the routine dread of returning home.

Vex returned from the gala in a daze. She walked to the back of the building rather than the front door, needing time for herself before going inside. Kneeling in the dirt beside a wilting foxglove, taking in the last sense of an untouched earth, a garden, a den of life, the calm before the fall.

Vex. The woman. Made me stop. Dead in the street. Saw her. Trust. Bit my tongue. Never mentioned. Stopped talking. So hurt. Wonder. Hell. In my head. Thought too much. Mind like hers. Certain light. Secrets. Honest. Loved her. Love her.

Vex left him a message. Park under the *ECSTASY OF THE VOID* billboard. Eric made a few drop-offs in the area in the past, but had never landed a long-term gig like this. Shot nerves. They made a stink about the billboard on the evening news. "Pornographic," they said. Eric heard the band got a mention in that article in Rolling Stone this month.

Long, flowing black hair. Black clothes. That's the end of his edge. Her style takes him by surprise. She dresses like Siouxsie but the glam is a deader—her face lurks under miles of makeup like she's her own mortician. But it's her body that's strange. Limbs too long, neck too long. Strange skin that seems to glow when the light hits her long. And slit pupils. *Must be contacts*, he thought. Vex and her pet beetle, Melville on a leash. Driving was never her thing. She needed the new hire.

Vex pops into the backseat, removing her leather

jacket, leaning forward against the partition. She notices the ankle strap of Eric's prosthetic.

"Familiar."

She sticks her hand though the middle of the partition. Eric turns and takes it in his. Vex' fingers are weighed down by so many rings, he can barely see her pale flesh under pale metal.

"I like you a lot more than my old driver already."

"The guy cause you trouble?"

"Shit, yeah. Dude was a downer."

"Well, I'll try my best to keep you happy."

She laughs.

"Where are you going tonight?"

"The Long Wharf Hotel."

"Seaside living?"

"You bet."

Eric turns the radio on.

"Any requests?"

"Any punk or new wave."

"Got it."

He turns the dial. Cocteau Twins. Pandora.

Vex rifles through her bag and pulls out a makeup compactor. She flips open the lid, revealing a light blue, glistening powder.

"Uh…?"

"Not a fan of Moon Dust?"

"Can't say that I am."

"Bad trip?"

"I never tried it. Friends have."

"Would you like to?"

Moon dust makes you see things. Real weird shit.

Eric holds up his hands in refusal. She snorts the dust, wiping some on her gums. It's the only that that makes her feel alive.

"No thanks. Not my kind of thing."

"Well, what is your kind of thing?"

Eric laughs, eyes on the road ahead.

"I just drive."

She could have said with acute assurance that the dreams began days before the dark pull, but her memory would never allow such pretense. There were imaginings in the preceding hours with particular frequency, but none as poignant and memorable as those of her youth. For almost two decades she had carried the burden of earth's expiration song. Shaken by the violence; the horror unmatched in fact or fiction. But she ignored it, and carried on. The somber ache found so often in the onslaught of human life had lost its appeal long before that day, but she felt the time had come to withdraw.

Vex Valis.

This is impossible! To be born in fracture, in segments. A mess, a monstrosity. There are only quiet corners for such a thing, to sit and contemplate the world as it is. And as it is, is not meant for me. I became lost in this gentle state. Preserved in my weakness as a sort of abstract strength. Only now, as the seepage seeps and the claws claw, dragging me out into the civilized world, do I realize how strange a thing I have become. I felt myself an animal dressed up in robes, making a mockery of existence as I step out to participate.

Nurses came in and out during the day to tend to Aaron's needs while Dr. Valis worked at the lab. The initial months of constantly being by his side had turned into years of slow inattention. It was not for lack of caring, but rather, a compelling need to find the solution to the very thing seeking to destroy him. One of the nurses had left the radio on as she always did. She switched it off and kneeled down to say an ordinary hello. He could not respond, or turn his eyes in her direction. Aaron had been incapacitated for four years at that point.

Friends used to visit, but their endurance faded. The husbands and wives of other afflicted scientists banded together for a time, but camaraderie fades in the onslaught of new responsibility. Dr. Valis found that forgivable. What she found unforgivable was the departure of their closest friend, Arthur. He was an old college classmate, enamored with the study of mysticism and occult artists. That was before the dissolution of the friendship.

Vex wiped the spittle from Aaron's mouth. His eyes, once brilliant, vibrant, had been overcome by a relentless fog. She could not bring herself to wonder if he was in that body any longer. Her heart told her so, and that was a greater horror than she could ever have conceived of.

There is a heated breath in the psyche of the evil, and it is, without a doubt, called indifference. It wasn't until Dr. Valis showed up late to the lab that fated day and saw Aaron through the glass door, convulsing on the ground. Dr Cristalen stood by the door, motionless. Within hours, Aaron's mind had been taken entirely.

Was she not doing her part to find a cure? Was that not a great service? She made peace at the time. It was not until duality began to ravage her that she began to doubt her decision. The sheath. It all circles back to the sheath.

Vex received a phone call from Dr. Cristalen on the Friday evening following the gala. She was incoherent, going on and on about a breakthrough. Vex assured her that she would be in early on Tuesday, after the Holiday weekend, as requested. The regular employees would be back to work by then and any study could be attended to with care. Ana insisted that she come immediately…

Ninety miles. Sweet girl. Different. Four years. Tough some. Without reason. Everything. Illness. Disappearance. Forgive her. Messy. Mistakes. Emotions. Better of me. Biggest regret. Say something. Baby girl.

They say they're working on a new album. Got a bunch of her Black Parlour pals to help her out the band. Eric heard her say something about a new chemical that she mixes in with the dust. She was never one for purity. He can't figure out why she has him park three blocks down from the entrance, either. Adds to the mystery, she says.

Vex runs out into the center of the street. It doesn't seem to her that she is anywhere special. Any sense of reality had been swept from her. Turning towards the building, she looks overhead to see a broken sign that reads, "Susurrus Studios."

Still covered in filth, she walks away from the hotel and down a barren city street in daylight, looking for Eric's car. A pleasant breeze swept from block to block, leading her onward. She walks a bit crooked; her back hurting. She has only recently woken up from deep sleep.

A worm pops up out of a garbage can.

"Gut ghouls?"

Vex lifts her coat and shirt, watching the cruel rippling beneath her torso.

"Still kicking."

The worm motions to spit. Vex jumps back, dodging the flow.

"What the hell!"

"It helps!"

She grabs the lid of the garbage can, aiming to smash the worm but it descends back into the grime before she can. Eric pulls up beside her. He rolls down the window.

"Have fun with your friends?"

"They aren't my friends."

"No?"

"They're pieces of shit."

"They can't all be."

He gets out of the car and opens the door for her. She stumbles slightly, refusing the arm he offers for balance. As he gets back into the car, he tries to change her mood.

"Listen, I'm sure you have at least one solid friend in there."

"Not in there."

He turns on the radio. Depeche Mode. Sister of Night

"So where are we heading?"

"How about your place?"

Vex loves because it is unfair. Unruly. Dangerous. What she loves is evil and it is not hidden from her in any context. She keeps on. She drinks she drives she fucks. They listen. To moans and groans and sounds of water on the roof. Untied ties and unzipped cocks, and papers in the morning that read "Thanks slut, I had my fun." She thinks he's that kind of guy.

Eric laughs. A surprised look slides across her face.

"Listen, kid. I'm divorced with two little ones. You aren't coming to my place. "

"Why? You think I'll be a bad influence?"

"I think you'll see the shithole I live in and yank my paycheck."

"I'd never do that."

"Nah. You're going home. "

Her eyes glisten.

"You know, they want to be around you 'cause their lives are shit. They just want something away from all that. Doesn't mean they don't genuinely like you. "

Vex pauses, thinking.

"I only have two real friends."

"Yeah? Tell me about 'em."

"Colette. She owns a bakery. Artsy type. Really quirky, but honest."

"She sounds cool."

"And Arthur. Used to be a scientist, smart as hell. Went to school with me and my husband."

Eric looks back at her through the partition, shocked.

"I didn't realize you were married."

"I'm not. He's dead."

"Oh…I'm so sorry."

Vex pulls out her compactor and dips her finger into moondust.

"Thanks."

"What about that Ana Cristalen they're always pegging you up against in the papers? Is that legit?"

"She's a legit cunt, sure."

Didn't let on. Long time. Felt. Vex. Couldn't provide. Not yet. Heat. Heat of the moment. Concern. Lose control. Responsible. Knew better. Pressure. Loving. Bullshit feelings. Good woman. Make the call. Hang up.

She never saw it coming.

When Dr. Valis arrived, the lab lights were on, but no one was there. She suited up, put on protective gear from her office. Did a quick sweep to make sure nothing was out of order. An array of things were out of place. Microbial samples were no longer contained. She knew why she had been summoned.

In addition to the release of the microbe sample, Dr. Valis noticed that whatever concoction Dr. Cristalen had formulated was been mixed and placed beside the sample. She left a bottle open. It wasn't going to take analysis to say that it was a lethal concoction. Dr. Valis walked to the leftmost cupboard and took out a vial of serum, volatile intentions affirmed. Footsteps. She left the lab through the eastern door, locking it behind her, snaking her way around the outer containment hall to the main door. Dr. Cristalen had entered the lab.

There are monsters in these sanctioned places. They have the look and obedience of the rest, but some lurking menace manifests eventually. Aaron had fallen to the malicious ambition of this woman. The gesture was not taken lightly. Dr. Valis locked the lab door shut behind her and sat down against the doorframe. She heard Dr. Cristalen, heard the distinctive plastic swish of the protective suit. She searched the lab thoroughly. The swishing became rapid. The clinking glass of test tubes joined in. And then screaming.

Dr. Valis stood up and looked out the window at the top of the door. The serum she left on the counter began oozing after exposure to the steam emitting from the mixture. Dr. Cristalen coughed violently, staring at her through the window. As the sound of hissing steam grew, she began knocking furiously. Dr. Valis pressed her ear to the door. For the first time since being introduced to Dr. C at the outset of the Transpermia Project, Dr. Valis felt a release of tension. Her head remained pressed to the cold metal, gradually getting warmer as the chemical atrocities collided. Dr. Cristalen begged as the door grew hot and the entire building rattled, but it remained locked.

"Open the door, Vex!" Where others may have given in, she stood firm.

"The door! The door!"

An explosion. All sound ceased.

Dr. Valis waited outside the lab for over an hour, sitting on the floor. Dr. Cristalen's body lay contorted and pale. A piece of strange matter sat on the counter, as thin as plastic wrap, glowing. Some kind of reaction between the mixtures and the microbes had taken place in the blast.

She spent several hours analyzing it when her eyes began to burn, marking the first symptom of exposure to the microbe. Frantically, she searched her suit for a weakness and found a tear beneath the right foot. Despite all precautions, she had been exposed. And yet, there she stood. The symptoms didn't progress as they did with the others. Assuming in her subtle derangement that the sheath-like anomaly was a neutral entity, and albeit harmless version of the microbe, Dr. Valis took it into the main lab and hung it in front of the southernmost wall. Weary of experiencing a version of the affliction with a delayed onset, she swallowed a tube of the "cure" serum she had been testing.

The fumes of Cristalen's chemical had not yet dissipated. As they washed over the translucent sheet-like sheath, it began to glow. It pulsed and emitted colors unknown to man. She was not in her right mind when she left the lab, or else she would have called the proper authorities. She returned home.

I am so alone in my oppression that I see nothing but abhorrence in the normal. What do I want? Do I want to slip back down to the shadow, where I will live long in the quiet safety of contemplation? Or will I step again, into the fire, risking life itself, so that I may live a moment, in exchange? This is the dilemma of a lifetime. Mine, which may be abbreviated in length and certainly so in breadth, is fragile. I do not know what to do with it. What to do with myself. I'd like to think the world itself teetering on fragile shoulders, its locks and limbs bereft with the strange odors of indifference. I want to think that nothing matters so that I may decline all things. And yet I bring myself to dilemma, in refusal of this very thing!

What a treacherous relapse she has descended into. She wanders through the Park and comes across those lethargic dancers Aaron once took photographs of for his gallery. She finds the one with the broken tooth and purple shall… that strange woman he used as a starting point for his photograph, Madam Marichov. She is generous enough to provide her with her old 'potion'. Liquid moon dust. The spell, the sweetest salvation, is upon her again. No hand but his forced her to the vial. A hand with the touch of fire. Sweet is the poison that captures the heart and disarms the body.

She closes her eyes and allows the knowledge of her stories to flow through her in the hope that, wherever they live, they may be written. *Spoken*. She stumbles home in that all-too-familiar transient despair. There is some strange glow outside her window. It sickens the mind to think of a scrap of light pervading the space. She thinks only of the single flame that crawled up the bath curtain as she soaked in lather. After years of quiet contemplation, she takes the dark plunge, reaching over to her dark medicine.

The most notable difference was her new and absolute deafness. That, and the absence of wind. The stillness disturbed her senses. As she tries to stand, she catches a glimpse of a tall moving object moving towards a strange, clotting river. Monstrous energies glide over her. Overbearing energy. Controlling energy. His energy. She knows the visual stench of the Eviscerator, always watching. Her dark meditation is interrupted by another worm.

"Gut gho…"

"Shut up."

Hell in her. Night. No friends. Tension. Fight. Morals. Regrets. Respect. Complicated. Attraction. Neglect. Pain in her. Quiet pain. Rogue wave. I remember. Dirt road. Broken glass. Storm through. Kneeling. Hold her.

Arthur's peculiarity was far advanced from the point of their previous encounter. His shoulders seemed permanently fixed to his earlobes, as though he had developed as everlasting state of alarm with the external world. But of his spirit and his framework, there was something far more concerning. His soul had gone fragile, and she knew that he was undergoing some great trial… or change.

Dr. Valis stared at him, unsure of his friendliness. The deeply-set wrinkles on his forehead and around his eyes were disconcerting. It looked as though he had aged fifteen years, not four.

"How's he doing? Arthur asked, newly returned from Cairo, trying to make amends.

"He's the same."

"I'm sorry."

"Yeah. Me too."

"What brings you by?"

"I saw Ana. On the news."

"Yeah. Tragic."

"Amazing that she manages to survive that."

Valis froze. She watched his eyes, knowing all too well his doubts about the merit of Ana's character. At the onset of the Transpermia Project, Arthur objected to them working with her because of her association with one infamous Dr. Collins and his inhumane diagnostic experimentation. Dr. Valis chalked it up to the intrinsic paranoia of the Von Aurovitch obsessives.

"Another tragic accident at the lab. Although I'm not sure why that would bother you."

"It certainly brought back old times. Old memories."

"Did it?"

An awkward silence passed between them. He had his prejudices, she had hers. Often she thought that he wanted her to find religion. Little did he know that given the choice between bible and blade, she chose the blade. To cut through nonsense and carve her own way, free of delusions of divine reward. It's not that it wasn't a novel idea. But to some, such comforts are so wearying that they are better left to those more inclined to lives devoid of cosmic contemplation. To be saved from this mess. What a lovely thing. And equally hopeless. In this blink of an eye called life, finding moments of the curious divine, but none so profoundly distinct that she could call herself a believer.

Gash. Remnants. Mangled metal. Soaked. Porcelain. Seaweed. Arms and legs. Shock. Hold her. Hell together. So vulnerable. Hold her.

You could do anything, write anything, sing anything, be anything, and you choose the life of the worm. There is a coward's nobility in that. At least I am not the dirt! Is that what you say? Oh, but the filth covers you. It is your refuge, your sanctuary. Never would you feel at ease in the sea of sky. Those places are too pure for you to writhe, or set about to ignite a firestorm of slime. I knew men so similar, too similar, that have brought fire to the altars of peaceful men. Violence as cleansing is violence as violence, have no doubt about that. Even a worm may bring about such selfish hardship to his brethren. Worms turn, and they also burn.

M ost of the time Eric drives her from the apartment in the north end to the recording studio. She didn't talk much the first week. Underneath the miles of presentation, Vex is deteriorating. He didn't anticipate feeling bad for her, but he does. Wednesday night of the second week, she calls him around dinnertime. She needs a ride from the show. It went bad, she says. Real bad.

He's waiting for her outside the Black Parlour Club. The Stooges. Rich Bitch, pouring out of the entryway. The whole crowd is decaying noveau-riche. It doesn't take him more than a few seconds to spot her. She has that glow. And that fur coat that makes her look like a fucking bear. She knows he can't stand that one. Vex takes it off and throws it to the car floor. Eric turns to look at her. She has a tiny leather dress on and a velvet harness. Where she finds this retro shit, he has no idea.

"Tonight's outfit is… Siouxsie or Bowie, I can't tell?"

"It's Vex."

"I see."

He turns up the radio. Bauhaus. The Passion of Lovers.

"I like your reference guide, though."

"Yeah, I peaked in the 80s."

"You?"

"Oh hey. Big hair, snake print leggings, the whole thing."

"You're shittin' me."

"Sadly not."

"You've got that aging cool guy thing going for you."

"Oh yeah. I'm really killin' it. "

He pulls onto the highway. After a few quiet moments, her curiosity stirs again.

"So what happened?"

Vex hesitates.

"I couldn't remember."

"The words? That happens to everyone."

"No. I couldn't remember… anything."

Eric looks at her through the rear-view.

"As in?"

"Where I was. What I was doing."

He shakes his head.

"Maybe lighten up on the moondust."

She rolls her eyes.

"You don't understand. I can't think without it."

This world was made for sinners. And not the kind of sinners defined in religious texts. I would delve into my advocacy of what I call "holy inversion," but think it ill-fitting to this day. The sinner's world, as we find it, is a world devoid of the kind of ethical consideration that can only be derived from a mind that has disconnected long enough from the modern world to contemplate the baseline states of cognition. One cannot, perhaps, be genuinely ethical without first experiencing human emotion. It is not enough to say one understands when one has not experienced. This brings us to the empathy deficit in modern man, an epidemic of sociopathy that topples any chance of ever developing a truly civilized world...

When Dr. Valis returned to the lab the next day, the sheath had grown to the size of a cottage window. She did nothing with it, save for monitoring the pulse rhythms and color changes. Her focus remained on the perfection of the serum, and the analysis of Cristalen's fuming potion. Analysis of both provided no clue as to the whereabouts of the remaining microbes. The majority of them had amalgamated into the sheath upon exposure to the two chemical mixtures, but a substantial amount remained missing. As for the serum, Valis had been able to hold off the rapid onset of her own illness, as long as she consumed a dose of the serum every six hours.

After thorough analysis of the chemical composition, she found that its toxicity levels were not suitable for oral consumption. It did, however, emit a red steam that, when inhaled, somehow illuminated the sheath. She made a note to study the sheath at the cellular level more adequately. If it was self-replicating or merely increasing in size would prove to be particularly important, but she needed to discover why the consumption of the substance had such an effect on its properties.

The growth of the sheath stagnated for a week or so, but it was not the only matter of note in the lab. Some organic growth was protruding from the side wall, along the only panel that is never touched by the sun. It had the look of a small tropical fungus. Further examination revealed its twin, no more than a meter apart on the same panel. Valis biopsied it and found that the genetic material seemed to be some hybrid variant of the alien microbe. In her altered state, she thought nothing of them on the first day. Not until they began to breathe.

We who wander beyond the Dome are the proverbial maggots of the compound. That infested soup they call culture has long been warped with thoughts of death and love of savagery without measure. What was I but a wandering child with eyes like thunder, watching men of supposed honor tear the veils of gorgeous women, behead their brothers, and poison wine and water in cups of blackest hue?

Several things haunted me back then. Several. One must say it with a roll of the tongue, or the essence of language is mislaid. Crisp air was not but a higher annoyance to my skin, and the smell of petrochor smothered me as I breached the outer wall of the city. For me, there is no greater prison than hunger. Some creation of man so vast that it blocks his view of the sun, the stars, the sky. It is what makes us man, is it not? Our hunger. Eyes must settle on the majestic natural world. Our bodies connect to the emerald realm, and wouldn't we learn from such harsh mistakes, such hopeless ventures, such unrequited love of some lurking creator?

Her stiff mohawk, unmissable in its shade of lazuli, looming overhead. A peculiar outfit, namely vinyl short-shorts and a distressed ruby crop top, turned almost as many heads as her hair. Underneath is a black fishnet bodysuit, torn in places that only give way during erotic exploits. All this under an oversized leather jacket with strange symbols sewn onto the back in glistening green thread. Tonight she has a show.

Vex wanders in the audience until she finds Arthur on the far right side, accessible seating. She plops down next to him, kissing him on the cheek. Eric lingers overhead awkwardly. He notices Arthur's limbs—they have the same strange elongation, the same sickly glow as Vex's.

"Eric, this is Arthur, Arthur, Eric."

The men shake hands and exchange niceties. Vex looks up to Eric.

"Are you going to sit?"

He sits on the opposite side of her, fidgeting with a beer. While the gear gets set up, the speaks blast *We Hunger*. Siouxsie and the Banshees. Vex turns back to Arthur, whispering.

Their eyes turn to the aisle as Ana Cristalen

approaches, grotesque opulence on full display. Eric is completely shocked by her. She is horrific—her exaggerated proportions not quite alien, not quite doll-like. He doesn't know what to make of her, but he can't look her in the eye. She slides into the seat behind him, her massive lime green plastic collar obscuring the senses, demanding their eyes scan its billowing mass. She directs her attention towards Vex, as always.

"Ecstasy of the Void will not be performing tonight."

"Uh… excuse me? Why the fuck is that?"

"Because Jerry over there…"

She smiles, waving her gaunt, spidery fingers at Jerry, a squamous blob of a stagehand. Her hands are covered by delicate leather gloves in muted turquoise, cracked like beetle shells under a stifled heel.

"Jerry will beat your brains out as soon as you finish your set."

Ana Cristalen twists her abnormally long neck around, scanning the audience. She stands and leaves. Vex remains silent. As the lights dim and the applause grows into maniacal roars, Eric motions to Arthur.

"Shall we?"

The three exit the theatre together.

"She is really fucking scary," Eric says. "What the fuck is wrong with her?"

"She's not her own person. " Vex answers.

An icy chill shot up Ana's spine and she was compelled to stand. She sat down again immediately.

"You… it didn't…"

"No, Miss. I am still quite alive. " Dr. Collins replied.

"You said the word. The disease."

"Indeed. It is only a word."

Spontanabre. The shock of hearing it faded, but Ana's mind spun with a fool's horror.

"If you've already discovered a cure, you must return and share your knowledge." She continued, composing herself.

Spontanabre. Another one on the hill. Spontanabre. The market place, in the vegetable aisle. They closed the store when they found that the grime, when mixed with fresh produce, created an immortal odor of lye and rotting meat.

"Why can you speak the word?" She asks him.

"Because it is not the word that destroys. It is what is behind it."

"Today the death toll reached one million people."

"Have you no idea who is compelled to say it?"

Ana pauses in confusion.

"Anyone who sees the affliction in progress."

"No. Those who possess... other traits."

"Far too many have died for that to be accurate."

"You are living in a shadow world. Whenever there arises some devilsome instinct, know this. Genetics will weed it out without pause. This is something that I dared not believe before. There is no darker cocktail than schadenfreude and the follies of greed and ambition."

"This is witch science." She replied.

"This is Darwin and the Divine at work together. Or something else, entirely."

They didn't speak for several minutes. Ana calmly returned to her original point.

"Von Auro..."

"Listen. Don't dwell so long in these dark places. They leave their mark. The portraits will be destroyed. As should the remainder of his works, but they are not mine to destroy."

"Your wife was dedicated to his work."

Collins, immediately consumed by sadness, became still. A cool breeze crawled through the lawn. Ana wrapped my white sweater tighter.

"Marcella was reeled in by psychotic darkness as many innocents are. I caught it too late."

"You know that many in the states blame you for the death of your daughter as well."

An ominous look bled through his face. For the first time, Ana felt the sting of panic.

"They are right."

Hours. Vex. Familiar pain. In the gut. Brutal night. Piercing hum. Verge of bursting. Pain of the stone. Ripping. Tearing mess. Acid. Nothing.

There's something about the gentleness of a December snowfall. It's the innocent end of winter, before the dark turn of the northern wind. Vex seems to like the romanticism of pre-Christmas revelry. The papers said she was a Satanist, so that surprised the hell out of Eric. Everybody has an opinion about Vex, but they don't see behind the scenes. The subtle crookedness to her walk from the pain in her ankles, the bags under her eyes, never eating, always vomiting and fucking, vomiting and fucking.

Sometimes it's like she's trapped in a snow globe, unable to take part in anything outside the fabricated scene of her containment. Eric used to envy that life. Not anymore.

The next morning is an early one. She doesn't look hung over, but she has huge sunglasses on that make her look like a bug. The radio is on. The Cure. *The Hungry Ghost.*

"Where to today?"

"The bakery on 6th."

Vex enters the empty bakery, TORTE DIVISION. The walls are hot pink, counters black, paintings of cute demons and psychedelic décor fill the small room. Tables and chairs are straight out of the 60s, cotton-candy pink. Colette emerges from the kitchen, blue hair back in a butterfly clip. She leans forward on the counter, cleavage nearly spilling out.

"Vex Valis, care for a taste?"

She reaches into the glass case and removes a small cake shaped like a penis. Vex raises an eyebrow.

"What did you hide in that one?"

Colette jokingly slams her fist on the counter. She grabs the cake with her bare hands, breaking it open. A cockroach crawls out and scuttles down the counter, hiding behind a salt shaker.

"There's only one kind of crunch like that."

Vex laughs. Melville, her pet beetle, crawls out from behind her hair and sniffs the cake crumbs.

"Daring little fella."

"You won't be cooking him."

"Nah. He's too loyal."

Vex turns to sit. Colette joins her. A bowl of dead

cockroaches and shattered crystals sit on the table. Vex takes a handful of the brittle bugs, chews and chews, spits them out onto the crystals. Pale beams of warm pink light shoots out in every direction, illuminating their faces.

"What brings you down this time?"

Vex places her summons on the table. Colette is no longer jovial. She stands.

"Downstairs, yeah?"

She walks behind the counter and through to the kitchen. Vex follows. They enter the walk-in refrigerator. Colette twists a stalactite in the far corner. A flaw in the wall reveals itself to be a door, opening with an icy crackling. Vex follows Colette down a cold stairwell to the hidden room below.

"The Eviscerator wants his delicacy. Guts and guts. But also, control of space, time, and all the dimensions," Colette begins to say, her own gut ghouls churning within her.

"How the fuck do you know that?" Vex asks.

"Hasn't Arthur read you that S Book Von Aurovitch bullshit? The only hope of stopping him, as you know, is…"

"Time dilation?" Vex answers, remembering Arthur's literary ramblings. Colette nods her head as she opens the door, revealing an enormous cavern housing thousands of strange clocks. Time-keepers from over a thousand worlds, procured through interactions with the sheath. Vex nods, and follows her down to the center of the cavern.

"Do you notice anything?" Colette asks.

Vex strains her senses.

"No ticking."

'Exactly. They've all stopped."

"When?"

"When this clock appeared."

They approach an enormous white clock that seems to have melted. The clock hands are made of matter inconceivable on earth. The numerals, alien to human intellect, a continuous pooling of black liquid by each indistinguishable numeral in the vast, hexagonal face behind glass. Vex stands before the clock in awe, running her hands over a set of characters on the outer edge that hasn't melted yet.

"Ulldythaer. I've heard this... somewhere."

"A dreaded place. Or so the Scaearulldytheraeum says."

Colette's energy is fading. She remains outwardly chipper, but the exposure to the clocks has taken a toll on her well-being. Who knows what toxic fumes they emit, or where they have been? They could be made of chemicals lethal to humans. They could have sat in toxic airs for centuries before being pulled through. Vex turns to Colette, marking her changing manner.

"Do you know who the Conspirator is?"

Colette smiles.

"I will note that you aren't asking me directly if it's me."

Vex smiles palely. Colette answers again.

"I know it's you."

The inevitability in the universe is that all things will return to chaos. This is the natural order. What one needs to do is examine chaos, and realize that humans have applied the negative aspects to it. Take mutation, for example. All living organisms are the result of genetic mutations. When we hear the word, however, we think of disease. We think of something negative. But mutation is a stepping-stone to intelligent life. Chaos is the emergence of life in embryo. It is Spontanabre. This concentrated chaos which yields organic matter is the magic of the universe. But its rarity and frailty need not cause alarm. We are but sparks in a vast darkness, immeasurable. We must deal with the problem of the average human being, who is, by nature, a neutral entity. They are no less and no more, but have utilized adherence and hierarchy to attain falsehoods designed by external tyrants. Structure is tyranny, although many refuse to believe that. All things, by nature, are meant to decay, to fail, to fall back into chaos. The pursuit of order will inevitably bring about disorder, because it is disorder that makes the difference. For individuals, for molecules, and for worlds. The truest truth ever born is that primordial gasp at the onset of inevitable chaos.

A few days after her initial discovery of the fungi, Arthur stopped by the lab. Valis left the main facility locked and met with him in the hallway. They exchanged the same awkward greetings as before, but judging from his expression, he still had not reached a point where he could get out whatever he had been meaning to say. The friendship had dissolved in fury years before, and his sudden resurfacing was just bad timing. After a slight pause, she once again remembered his papers, his fascination with mythology. Perhaps, she thought, if she interjected a little something about the sheath, he would say what he had been meaning to say.

"Can you see it?" She asked him.

"See what?"

"The sheath."

He looked in through the window.

"I see… edges. Blurriness. Clear, then indistinct."

"Incredible. Sometimes it becomes brilliant opalescent blue. It pulses, like an organ," she said, watching his reaction. A look of horror came over his face, then sank just as quickly into calm.

"Strange."

She continued. "I haven't figured out the pattern behind the rhythm yet."

"Is that something necessary to study?"

"Excuse me?"

His tone changed.

"Shouldn't you be spending more time with Aaron? He seems to be in the final stages. And you... don't seem well either."

Her throat ached in the fury of holding back an honest, reaction.

"Leave."

Having been cured of niceties in grad school, Valis left him in the hallway and returned to the lab. He didn't need to know how strong her dedication really was.

Another week passed. The sheath began as a thirteen by thirteen centimeter square. By then it took up the space of the entire wall, some six by nine meters. Valis continued to consume the serum, making minor adjustments in the components in order to examine its effectiveness. She also continued making adjustments to Cristalen's mixture in order to analyze the steam emissions and its impact on the sheath. This second serum also had a separate power. It inflicted some fascination with the sheath that could not be fought by will alone. She crudely began referring to the serums as yellow (the cure) and red (the aggressor of the sheath).

Despite its alluring presence in the lab, Valis made a point of keeping her distance from it. That was, until the day when the red emissions consumed her psyche so fiercely that she did something that she never would have done in her right mind... just a slight taste. Valis let three droplets drip down her teeth, past her tongue, and swallowed. The sheath glowed with a particular fury and luminescence that she had not yet seen. Valis approached it. The constant rippling and pulsing of the organic material felt calm near her face. Against all better judgment and under the influence of the serum, she reached out to it and laid the palm of her right hand against its surface. Everything went black.

There is no shade of black darker than that of the other side. Tales of azure and opulent gates become a distant recollection once one is bombarded by the imminent absolute- tales of salvation were decorations of a mind haunted by mortality. And yet, this place, though not found in theology, was indeed somewhere. Vex listened as the sounds of billions of voices drowned into some invisible vortex above her. She floated, and forgot, and told herself that these dark imaginings were the result of the brain shutting down for eternity. As the weight and density of a once-precious Earth barreled down upon her head and memories of life became tendrils of fading smoke, she once again felt the pull and wavered in and out of conscious in a vortex of pale grey dust. As the particles acquired a burnished hue, she lost consciousness completely.

There are whispers from lost worlds, melancholy invocations, that seek us out to remind us of our personal haunts. These whispers grow louder in every dream.

Valis woke up and saw nothing but red light. She was no longer in the lab, couldn't even tell if she was still in her body. She looked down to see that the pressure differential of wherever she was had become so vast that her flesh had turned to globs. Suddenly a strange light ripped away what appeared to be cylindrical tiles from some intangible dome overhead, and she could see purple plasma floating outside. For a few seconds, the material of the dome ceased its rippling to reveal iridescent lakes floating in mid air, and pink rays of light raining down like some supernatural, triangular object. That's when the pain began.

Valis felt stabbing sensations in the side of her torso and shoulders. Then, feeling like she had been struck by lightning, was thrust backwards into the blackness, back into the lab. She woke up on the floor, covered in sweat. The sheath was no longer colorful. She slowly stood and stumbled to the main station for a dose of the serum. It was far too early for it to be necessary, given the measurements. She looked at the clock to see that six hours had passed. Six hours, and yet she had only been gone for mere minutes. Questioning her sanity, Valis shut off the lights and rushed home.

As she walked up the stairwell in her apartment building, Valis was accosted by a flashback of a jagged metallic tool on an organic wall tearing at her torso. She stopped and lifted her jacket to find a scar, and toyed with the idea that the wound was a manifestation of a psychic manipulation from the chemical assault, rather than the onset of the affliction. She would know soon enough. This was not a solitary manifestation. Bruises, scrapes, and rashes of strange textures appeared within the next twenty-four hours of her entry into the sheath, all where she had been stabbed by unseen blades.

CAT scan. MRI. Ultrasound. Guts. Edges. Damp things. Vex. Vanish. Pain. Lost. Bird. Pacing. Sky bleeding. Curious sight. Dreaming of life. My fault. Obsession. Not hers. Unnatural. Absolute. Always here.

Eric didn't anticipate liking her that much. He expected to bite his tongue every day, tending to the whims of a bitch, but that was so far from the reality. Vex was sweet. Delicate, even. Every bit of information he found to prepare for the job had been misleading. It was all fake. A persona designed for public consumption. Part of that was comforting. She wasn't a rock star. She was painfully human.

Every once in a while Vex would give him a little snippet of her life behind the studio doors. He dropped off some things to her a few times, usually when no one else was there. One time she sat him down to show him the switchboard. She seemed to like having him around. It never took him more than fifteen minutes to start edging his way towards the door.

"So where am I schlepping you to today, Miss Thing?"

"Just… here."

She hands Eric a slip of paper with an address on it, written in the worst chicken scratch he'd ever read.

"This your writing?"

"It's shit, I know. Let's get going."

"You ok?"

"I have a headache."

"I'll tint the windows for you."

He shuts off the radio.

"Thanks."

Eric takes her to the far end of the city. The area behind the hospital is s a bit unfamiliar, but he knows there are old studios in the back end. Eric parks beside one of the brick warehouses and reaches for the door.

"Let's just wait here. I need a minute."

He leans back in his seat.

"Take all the time you need, kid. I'm here with you."

Vex wipes the tears out from under her sunglasses. Eric opens the glove compartment and hands a few tissues back to her.

"Thanks."

"You got it."

Sexual contact. The sights, the smells, the textures, the fluids. There is no defilement greater than carnal "pleasure," which should rather be described as feeding. But there is not only this revilement at the deed. There is a sharp, panging boredom. But it feeds the hunger. I'm bored with gums and bodies. But this Boredom eau de Grotesque does not originate with touch, despite my immediate cringing at outstretched extremities. It begins with one of one particular glaze over the eyes of an exhausting party. Suitors, they are my seaweed unicorns. And I wish to drown them all. But I need them.

Bloody thighs are her only sun. She fucks hard and fast, loving the abuse of it. The stranger pulls her to his pelvis, his hands wrapped around her hips. Her nightgown, caught up around her breasts, slides further up over her face. He tears it away. Her nipples press against the wood table, hardness on hardness. When his cock penetrates her, she lets out a sigh of relief. It is a respite, to be fucked so mercilessly in the peak of the August heat. Within seconds they are both soaked in sweat, sliding on each other's flesh.

"Come back tomorrow."

Vex doesn't answer.

"You want to."

She turns away from the stranger, towards the window, overlooking the skyline. His room, on the top floor, is one of the highest in the city. She doesn't like looking out.

"I'll have to see what I end up doing tomorrow."

She wasn't lying. There was a show coming up.

"I want you back here."

Vex, silent and expressionless, slides the handle of her purse over her shoulder.

"Thanks."

Switch one way and she doesn't have to worry about control anymore. Switch the other, and she calls the shots. In that way, she can never lose, yet still somehow always does. Not with Arthur. All is gentle there.

Tired by her cerebral winter, she flees again to him—eyes glassy, cheeks pale. She and Arthur lay in a quiet embrace on the floor of his apartment, her legs wrapped around his peculiar stumps, arms locked, heads touching. She clings to him like a drowning man clung to crumbling rocks. Vex won't put words to the feeling, but it's the only feeling that makes her live longer. The only one worth living for. Arthur gets it.

He moves a lock of hair out of her face. Staring into her eyes, he relieves himself of the burden of admission for a moment. Music is playing. Echo and the Bunnymen. *In Bluer Skies.*

"Colette said something about the S Book." Vex says, pressing her nose against his cheek. Arthur shifts.

"Yeah."

"What is that about? Time dilation?"

He sits up, reaching for the arm of his wheelchair for balance.

"I can't discuss that with you."

"Why the hell not?" she asks, desperation growing wild within her.

"Because you're the Conspirator."

Vex sits up. She hunches over in agony, immediately overcome by belligerent gut ghouls. They attack her insides with unknown fervor, gnawing and gnawing until she is lost in pain-delirium. They've finally reached her bones.

"I am."

A stronger gust makes its way up the street and manages to blow several flyers off of utility poles. She approaches the papers on the sidewalk. Leaning slowly, feeling pressure in her head, she picks one up and sees a familiar face…her face.

She says her name aloud, unconvinced that she is the same girl she sees in the image. It seems to have been taken ages before, despite being a recent picture. She had become a different being since that time, and had done so in a matter of moments. How it had happened, she has no recollection. She crumples up the paper and throws it down a storm drain, into the sewer, thoughts turning to Arthur and Colette. If the Secretarium finds out they are helping her, they'll be dust dust dust. Looking up the street, she decides to try and reach the park. It's a long walk; it will take her until nighttime to get there. The sun looms overhead, marking midday. She decides to walk as far as she can, and rest wherever she can at dusk. In a world devoid of activity, there is an eerie sense of danger in the prospect of darkness. She is determined not to expose herself to any more dangerous lurkers of the night.

FARAH ROSE SMITH

"The Worm King would like to see you."

Vex turns to see a peculiar worm, bright purple and larger than the others, sitting on a stoop.

The worm plops down onto the sidewalk and sits at her feet.

"Will you see him?"

"Are you going to spit in my face again?"

The worm shakes his head in refusal. Vex thinks for a few minutes, unsure of the best course.

"Can he help me with the Eviscerator?"

"Yes!"

"Well, sure, what the fuck."

"Has anyone you loved ever been sick, Dr. Cristalen?"
"My mother."

The first time Ana saw the power of illness was the way it wrapped itself around her mother's mind. There is no greater horror than to look into stare of those you love, knowing that the great tome of their life has become a blank page.

"Then you know. You would do anything. Anything."

"To see them right again."

They pause as a quiet breeze travels around the corner of the château, mushrooms swaying, floral scents stirring her into an involuntary daze. Dr. Collins continues.

"I thought Marcella found some solace in his work. Some reflection of her own suffering. I didn't know how much had been eaten away."

"Until you looked."

"Until I truly looked, yes. Far too late."

"Listen. We can't control fate. And we can make all the wrong choices and betray everyone we love. But it doesn't change the end game."

"That, my dear, is where you are wrong."

She pauses.

"But you don't want to find the cure?"

"That is your end game, Dr. Cristalen. Not mine."

"Do you sleep, Dr. Collins?"

He smiles darkly, taking a sip of his black tea.

"Rest has been a foreign concept to me for some time."

Ana waits for him to place his cup back on the saucer.

"Do you decline the pardon?"

"Yes. " He answers, without hesitation.

"But why? Don't you want to go home?"

"Don't you know what I have done?"

Ana becomes truly afraid. She freezes in her seat, suddenly aware that all natural life—birds, bugs—has grown silent around them.

"I have no desire to return, or to investigate this affliction. It seems to me that the matter escaped the confines of medical practice."

"A cure must be found, or…"

"Or what? Those inclined to shout the word will fall. Those who are blind to the ways of the world, and see fit to assign accusations. I have no further interest."

"You refuse to participate in finding the cure, and you burn the only chance of finding one. Von Aurovitch…"

"Any devotee of Von Aurovitch knows of his deeply entrenched obsession with exotic alchemy. He was a man of art AND science. The most dangerous breed of all."

"Are you not one of these men?" She interjects, without caution.

"I am not an alchemist. I am a doctor."

"You were a doctor."

"I am not like Von Aurovitch. What kind of man do you think I am?"

"Did you know that the first documented case of the affliction occurred only a few miles away from your estate outside of Berlin? An item was found there. A metal briefcase which belonged to Von Aurovitch. It was purchased by you several weeks before at auction in Paris."

He stops cold. He speaks again, more to himself than to her.

"Marcella always said, if you want to know someone's character, don't show them something nice. Show them something terrible. And then watch their eyes."

Ana stands up, gathering her coat and briefcase. He remains seated.

"Did you think I would not be able to tell why I was being summoned to the States? Then let's skip right to the reality of this meeting, shall we? No. I am not the Godfather of Spontanabre. It is not mine, by hand or mind, or invention."

"You fell from quite the height of society, sir."

"Without grace or privacy, I might remind you. Which is one of many reasons why I don't have a television."

"You must understand that the breadth and scope of this pandemic makes you subject to international law. It's only a matter of time before the French authorities make their move."

"I am not the culprit behind this, and you know it." He says.

Ana hesitates, sitting down again.

"I believe you. But more questions must be asked. By people with far more understanding.

"Oh, I believe you understand me."

Discomforting chills, knees knocking, hands

fidgeting. She doesn't know what to do.

"Why don't you tell me of your own fascination with Von Aurovitch?" Her head shoots up, shocked.

"Pardon?"

"Tell me."

A dark match, they were. The betrothal of the knife and vine. Marcella was a beautiful creature, but a haunted one. Haunted by the injustices that often infect one sheathed by the mask of beauty. She hid her illness well from the world. Just like Goethern's blue lady. But Ana was something else. Something that could be useful to him.

"My only commitment to Von Aurovitch is aiding the destruction of his collections. What is your interest, young lady? Why might a scientist have become involved?"

"What happened?"

"Sadistic machinations parading as art. Monstrosity on canvas. It's all fascinating, isn't it?"

"Obsession, then."

Ana nods

"How far have you delved into his scientific theories? The diseases in the S Book?" he asks. "Has your research touched upon any of the others?"

Vex descends the pipes, following behind the worm. Slime cakes the passageway, smelling of petrified vomit and sewage. Hundreds of young worms gather the slime in tiny buckets.

"What are they doing that for?"

"Juice! Good juice!"

It leads Vex to a deep cavern in the sewer, putrid and odorous. The Worm King looms overhead, dangling from a rusty bronze rod, his robe of scarlet dragging through the atmosphere on invisible ridges. Curious sigils appear in the muck beneath him and vanish as quickly. His attendee, Larinkge, in normal hours thriving as a mere mushroom, transfigures into a tall human figure made entirely of glass. Vex recognizes a great bulge of light and, with half-closed lids, dark with soot, sits down in a sorrowful confusion before them. She empties her mind of confusion and listens. The worm king sputters sounds inconceivable to human ears. Larinkge translates.

"You have received a summons from the Eviscerator, yes?"

"I have."

"And when must you meet with him?"

"Not sure yet."

Larinkge informs the Worm King of her answers. A deep shudder runs through him and he drops down from the bronze rod, unfurling to his full height, pus rolling down his robes. A procession of small worms approaches, balancing buckets of white, bubbling sludge. Larinkge cups the liquid in their hands and holds it to Vex's mouth.

"Drink."

"Fuck no!"

"It is the only way to silence the ghouls."

Vex remembers the internal gentleness that sank in after the worm spit in her face weeks before. She reluctantly touches her tongue to the unctuous milk and tastes. The power over her in the form of white drops. She has forgotten how sweet the taste is. Slowly it comes back to her.

She waits and waits, until she is strangely overcome by the ancient ache of a human mind in existential disarray. Then it comes. She jerks forward violently. A strange slurring of the senses! The last thing she witnesses comes in the form of floating metal, as though gravity had been deleted from Earth's arsenal of life-nurturing implementations. That is when she feels the pull.

Vex is unconscious and floating ever-so slightly off of the ground. Memories float out of the caverns of her mind, she hears strange whispers from the darkest depths of her subconscious. A fractured memory of a planet covered in grey cliffs and dark green oceans grew. As she breaks apart into the cosmic nothingness, she sees life, hears life, sitting on a cliff on this world of sick oceans. She the screams of the monstrous immortal, agonizing stories. Her story.

You are not listening.

Vex winces.

"It works," Larinkge answers. "You will take a bottle with you, and the worms will deliver several barrels in time for your visitation."

"What for?"

The worm kind shudders again, leaning close to Vex's face. She remains entirely still, unsure of the countenance of worms. It emits a horrid sound, spraying pus over her. She cringes in disgust. Larinkge continues.

"Wormjuice is the only thing that will destroy the Eviscerator. You must soak him in it. "

Vex, astonished, shakes her head.

"That is impossible."

"Improbable!" A small worm yells up at me. "Only improbable!"

Dr. Valis woke up the following day in agony. She took the yellow serum. It took over an hour to gather the will to enter Aaron's bedroom to check on him. She received a phone call from her friend Katherine, a former lab tech whose husband had been one of the victims of the affliction. She invited her to a neurology symposium, but she declined. No one had yet seen her in her present condition. If they did, they would know she had been exposed. Besides, the social sphere was the poison apple of her fairy tale. Valis could never submit herself to such occasions without angst. All the eyes, all the hands. All the mouths moving in a discordant opera of judgment. Deprive her of the social sphere and she would have, in earnest, grow to profound heights. Without distraction. Without fear.

Valis decided to stay away from the lab that day. She was unable to stand upright for long without a sharp ache in her stomach. Instead she retreated to the small garden she had been permitted to plant in the back of the building. In the garden, after tending to endless dead weeds and dead roots, she sliced her finger on a jagged rose thorn. She lifted her hand close to her eyes, still burdened by blurriness, and saw that the blood was sky-blue.

Here, sinking into the moldy bank of the black river, in a humid fog unlike any known in a livable world. Here. Maniacally twisting trees, moaning branches, swaying weeds. Skies of violent emerald and mud of battered coal. Every second was a struggle to stay conscious as the smell of slurry suffocated my senses. I crawled away from the river, afraid of the kind of life that might erupt from such waters, and stood up beneath an alien willow tree. It stood on a tall embankment overlooking the vast terrain that looked so precisely designed, despite its grotesquery, that it could only be described as a garden of the immortal macabre. No more, of these horrid dreams…

When she returned to the lab, Valis saw that the twin fungi had grown significantly. They were now each the size of tomato soup cans, and moved back and forth at will. In her right mind, she would have had them removed immediately, but in the aftermath of the "experiment-gone-wrong" and given her own slow decline after various chemical exposures, she let them be. She began to mix that week's batch of serum. As she let it process, Valis felt the all-too-familiar sensation of quiet accompaniment. She was not alone. Out of the corner of her eye, she thought she saw a faint protrusion in the sheath that quickly retracted and disappeared within the constant rippling. Valis chalked it up to an onset-hallucination and ignored it.

She left the lab soon after. For once, she wanted to be home. After dark she wheeled Aaron out onto the balcony with her. She looked through the telescope and saw purple plasma in the sky. Tendrils appeared, reaching out to nearby stars and expanding its influence over the vacuous surrounding arena. Its color was more saturated. The manifestation of anomalies in interstellar space was far beyond the reaches of her specialty, but she continued to look into her findings. Small comfort came in the form of pursuing a classification that would negate the matter from being a sheath-induced hallucination. She received no such comfort from her brief study or the consultation of literature. The Eviscerator, first glimpsed with some dark renown in the firmament. Climbing high, beyond the distant stars. The lord's perversions bloom on earth through forgotten doors, tooth by tooth and star by star.

Valis looked at Aaron, wanting to tell him. Wanting him to hear. She touched his face and wheeled the telescope over to him, angling the viewfinder to his eye and holding it still, in case he could catch a glimpse in the waves of mental static—his prison.

The sheath didn't grow any larger, but that was of no consequence. It was enormous. Valis wondered if her "entry" had something to do with it. Like a spider web, built only large enough so that it may catch its prey. She entered the lab and heard wheezing coming from the corner. The fungi had doubled in size, and small dark openings had formed on the extreme front of their form. They were pulsating. She uttered one insignificant profanity. Their breathing slowed. The fungi, in unison, turned towards her. They had no eyes, but they knew she was there. Of that, there was not a doubt in her mind. She remembered as a child, standing in empty rooms and hearing some intangible thing breathing beside her ear. Fear hadn't crossed her mind at the time. She felt sorry for it. Some broken life in some unknowable place rained its sorrows down upon her, and she could do nothing. Someone with their wits about them would have left the room to hell in that moment, but her hell was home and she could bear it no longer. She could not bear the burden of that promise. In direct opposition, Valis continued to search for the cure.

Lost in painful memories again, she accidentally took a dose of the red serum instead of the yellow. Her ears pulsed in pain. Sounds were drowned out by a crackling whir, like the sounds of a radio losing a signal in a storm.

Valis turned around to see that the sheath had turned a deep sea-green, unlike any shade it had previously emitted. Feeling a surge of irrational daring, as some so often do in psychological distress, she reached out to it. Once again, all went black.

She was in again. This time the cathedral dome encasing her was a murky blue-green. It had retained its usual translucent wall, but this time what looked like yellow veins pumped some unknown liquid throughout. The walls pulsed. Her body was no longer a pile of globular matter, though it was far from its normal manifestation. The humidity of the enclosure was unbearable. She toyed with the idea that she was sitting inside an organ in the digestive system of some unknown life form. That theory was quickly shot down when the walls of the dome turned clear and she sensed she was being watched. A great blade tore through the ceiling, raining down red light and pus onto her. She began to choke on it, and was once again pulled violently backwards. Valis was thrown back into the lab.

When her eyes opened, she was covered in yellow pus. She had hit her head on the lab bench. This time, the clock indicated that she had, true to form, only been gone for several minutes. Her limbs seemed to have elongated. She struggled towards the sink to wash away the scum. Her teeth ached in a manner suggesting they might have been individually twisted in the gum and then shoved further in...

I had a dream last night, in my wretched confinement. It was the death of Marcella that led me to the thought of the Dome. In that original state of horror, there was little room for such reflections. I left my home with the intention of meeting death in the deep forest beyond the crimson river. His eyes had beckoned me long before she succumbed. He teased me through her pallor, her misty gaze and speckled skin. What once were gentle freckles turned to weeping sores. Is beauty to die such a mournful, grotesque death without cause? Never had I met such an ungainly faculty as possessed by this raven-haired girl. With a mind to miss a doorway and trip on the stairwell, she did so as a deity. No one laughed at her. Her presence was too great. Her eyes too deep. She was, in every sense of the word, an angel amongst men. I did not know she was the wolf. I did not know she was the wolf. And I, the herald of the Eviscerator…

Vex doesn't want to believe in any future that doesn't empower her, but the days roll into each other. The same narrative of obedience, work, drugs, and travel. Eric doesn't know how she stays awake. It's got to be more than moon dust, he thinks. That shit… it puts you to sleep as soon as the faeries start dropping out of the sky. He doesn't know from experience, only heard of the hallucinations.

He didn't see her with moon dust after the first day, but he knew she was doing something. She was never quite right when she got into the car. Always under the influence. She dealt with the pressure that way. The commitments she'd made to others far outreached her strength. He doubted anybody said as much. To them she was a work horse. She never showed them any less. But when she got into the car, that was always a different story.

Vex is aggravated. He hasn't seen her that run down so early in the morning before. The show the night before was garbage. Eric can tell his usual methods of trying to cheer her up aren't going to cut it. He isn't curious about the drugs initially, or rather wasn't going to pry, but finds himself closer and closer to a few questions. She seems to be getting worse every time she gets into the car. Each day brings a new depth to her pallor, a new vein popping out of her skin like a rope ready to snap. The bones in her chest are visible, her curves are gone. He doesn't know if she's anorexic or on coke, but it's something. And the closer they become, the more it scares the hell out of him.

Talking Heads. *Stay Hungry*.

"Hey, Vex."

"Hey, Eric."

"No good today?"

"No good."

"Anything I can do to help?"

"I don't know."

"Well, where are you off to?"

"Appointment, recording session, whatever."

"And how much time do we have 'til then?"

"Why?"

"Well, any time for a detour?"

"Uh…"

"Twenty minutes. You have twenty minutes?"

"Yeah, I have that."

"Good. I wanna show you somethin'."

"Sorry, I left my…"

"Magnifying glass at home, yeah I've heard that one." She laughs.

He drives her out of the city. It takes much longer than twenty minutes, but she makes no mention of it. She seems happy, throwing her schedule to the wind for a few hours. Eric pulls up to the old spot and opens her door. She gasps.

"Never seen nature's end of the city?"

"Never."

"Well, here you are, Miss Valis."

"Holy shit."

Few people make it out to the end of the river, but Eric always found it worth the drive. The lake is massive, reminiscent of the old lake up in Maine where he grew up. Vex takes off her shoes and throws them in the back of the car. She runs up to the water and sticks her feet in. She starts laughing.

"Not bad, eh?"

"Cold as shit, but fuck. This is beautiful."

"Yeah."

"How did you find it?"

"One of my joy rides."

"I wish I had time to swim."

"Well, you can come back."

"We can?"

"Sure."

He can't figure out if she is asking for permission or asking if he'll come with her. Either way, Eric wanted her to know there was something else out there, other than cold steel.

The ride back is quiet. She's peaceful. The usual anxiety Vex projects is decidedly absent, until they reach the highway.

"I wish I could stay out there forever."

"You could build a cabin."

"Ha! They'd still find me."

"A cabin with a really big fence."

"Then I couldn't see the lake, and there would be no point."

"True."

"Maybe when I'm old and bald and withering, they'll let me be."

A few silent moments pass. He pops a CD into the player. Dead Can Dance. Children of the Sun.

"Sorry for mixing up your schedule."

"Fuck it. Totally worth it."

"Good to hear."

"Hey…"

"Yeah?"

"Thanks."

"No need to thank me. I just…"

"Drive, yeah."

"Mmmhm."

Vex looks out the window, smiling to herself. It's an honest smile.

Waking. Pour heart. Loathsome. Alone. Never know. Forgive. Instincts. Death. Dying. Wonder.

When Dr. Valis arrived home that night, she found Aaron lying awake in his bed. Realizing that in her confusion she had left the yellow serum in the lab, she remained hunched over, guarding her abdomen. The affliction routinely took thirty-six hours to fully manifest, so she was faced with finding a way to gather her strength and return to the lab. Even the weight of her clothing was abrasive to her newly-frail skin. The phone rang in the hall. She hobbled out and picked up the receiver.

"How are you?" A voice asked.

"Who is this?"

"Arthur."

Valis rolled her eyes. "Don't you mean how is Aaron?"

"How are both of you?" His concern sounded honest, but she was too tired to maintain her usual emotionless approach. His newfound concern made no sense to her. "Well, we're alive."

"Vex."

"Look, I don't have time."

"I didn't really get a chance to say…"

He stopped, gathering his will, or bravery, or something. He began.

"Have you spoken to Dr. Cristalen lately?"

She inhaled sharply.

"No. Should I?"

"Vex, there's something wrong with her. She's not herself."

"I wouldn't think so."

She hung up, leaning her head against the wall. Gravity was a growing burden, and her ability to reconcile its pull became more difficult than ever. She went back into the bedroom, and was suddenly compelled to remove her clothes. She lay down next to him. He was worse. So much worse.

She had promised him that she would end it. Valis kept it alive in her mind that his torment would be ended with a cure. A cure that she was able to find herself. She could not end it as he had told her to. She fought against herself, trying to keep from imagining the completion of the task. In her mind, it would never come to pass. If she had thoughts upon the matter, they would never have illustrated this descent; this parallel agony. In this way, she was reminded of her own arrogance. Her knees buckled under the weight of her new-found height. Her skin had begun to peel in some strange way mimicking a radiation burn or chemical exposure, giving way to muddled maroon. She tried to sleep, but remained awake. Tried to listen, and heard only static. She chewed and chewed, and her jaw was never rested. She had never been so utterly alone.

Valis woke to find that more than enough hours had

passed for her to be eternally incapacitated, but she still had not succumbed to Aaron's affliction. She tended to him quickly and threw on her newly undersized clothes, rushing to get to the lab. When she arrived, she found that the fungi were now quite large. They had grown extraordinarily long, sharp teeth, but still no eyes. That endless sense of being watched, however, only grew more intense.

Valis mixed up a batch of yellow serum quickly. Despite almost two decades of education that beckoned her to wake from this hellish trance, she sat on the bench and drank it down. As she waited for it to take effect, she heard some telepathic whisper from the sheath. It hung there—motionless, colorless, beckoning her to bring it to life. Consumed by this new aberration of thought, a malodorous trance, she mixed the red and drank it.

Not unlike the perils of an addicted brain, Valis was overcome by the need to re-enter the sheath. She fought herself, attempting to grab onto the lab bench, but it toppled over as she continued lurching forward. The sheath undulated and glowed in colors she had never known. She cringed as she was thrust head-first into the rippling.

The room was no longer domed. In fact, it had no visible overhead whatsoever. Merely an endless set of four walls climbing to unknown heights and disappearing beyond teal gas. Above her, two vast manifestations of translucent organic matter passed over in specific rhythms.

A strange sensation washed over her limbs. An ecstasy not rare on earth in type, but perhaps in manifestation. The walls became transparent, exposing a strange horizon soaked in colors unperceiveable to human eyes. The rhythmic pulsing of the organisms seemed to be the focal point of the endless landscape. In that strange ritual she acquired some forsaken knowledge. Hallucinations and dreams of the birth of the universe in cyanotype. Knowledge she had never possessed flooded into her mind. The more she knew, the more afraid she became. It was unbearable. She heard the infinite whispers of some profound malevolence, hovering in every corner of the room. A shadow moved closer, objects in hand, indecipherable in the confusion of the fetid dreamland. Valis felt one sharp slice to her stomach and the removal of her organs. Screams rang out from impossible distances, back into herself. She was expelled by the sheath for the third time...

There's people in history—even today—who elevate the beautiful in death. *Well, fuck them,* Eric thinks. There's nothing good about a beautiful thing wasting away. It's more than circumstantial decay. When someone's life force gives way to the grey inevitability, you feel it in your guts. Eric felt it, and he'd barely known her for more than a month. Only a monster could look at what was happening to Vex and try to elevate it to some kind of art form. Real death isn't art. It's a fucking horror. But it's all the glory to the ignorant, even when the vulnerable are gutted. How the fuck did people like that start doing well in this world? They wear their thousand dollar suits to their thousand dollar dinners, and barely have two thoughts outside of their next reckless acquisition. Just like Ana.

Midnight. Ana Cristalen shows up at the door in all black. A strange pallor differentiates her from the papers. It's unsettling. Vex wonders about her resurrection. About her loyalty to the Eviscerator. The thought of her being ill was somehow too painful to bear, even though she hated her.

"Come in."

Ana takes a few steps into the parlor and looks around.

"May I take your coat?"

"Actually I won't be long, Vex."

"Oh?"

Vex feels a jolt from the gut ghouls that nearly knocks her over.

"I need your help with something."

"Not gonna hit me first, huh?"

"This isn't really a funny thing."

"Ok."

Ana walks into the living room, removing her coat. She sits in the red velvet armchair. Many a night Vex sat in that chair, thinking about Ana, and the night of her death. She struggles to ground herself in the reality of the moment. Vex sits opposite her on the couch.

Her favorite Sisters of Mercy record is on the turnstile. *Black Planet* starts playing as Ana begins.

"Do you ever wonder how things might have been different?"

Vex freezes, unsure of how to respond honestly. Of course her mind had indulged in endless fantasies about salvation, some of them more shameful than others, but none of them were ever thought of with the intent to hurt anyone. Only to save Aaron, Colette, Arthur, herself…

"No."

Ana smiled.

"No guilt, eh? You're still a terrible liar, Vex."

"I'm not lying."

"Not in full, no. Not this time."

Ana looks down at the floor, trying to hide her face from Vex as she always did when it war revealing too much.

"You never got the full account. Of what happened."

"About you killing my husband or you coming back to life?

"About the Eviscerator."

Vex sits up, shifting her body in an attempt to calm the surging pain of the gut ghouls. She can't remember if she's sipped any wormjuice yet tonight.

"What exactly do you mean by that?"

Ana stays quiet, watching her closely. The old fury is growing stronger. Vex remains calm.

"Girl, you have the balls to dance around this one, do you?"

"No. Not anymore."

Vex stares, trying not to reveal the hurt.

"You know, it took me a lot of years… a lot of

years… to wrap my head around what the hell happened back then, and what I came up with still don't make any god damn sense. The only thing that makes sense to me is the end of it."

"And?"

Ana stands, walking towards the window.

"I wanted to tell you before. I wasn't able to stay close to you then. After we…"

"Fucked?"

"No, shut up about that!"

"Ana, I'm tired. Real god damn tired. Just get at it, because I am telling you, after this night, I am done with your bullshit!"

"You are the conspirator."

A cold shiver has a chokehold on Vex's throat. Fear descends into calm resolve. Ana continues.

"You are conspiring to destroy the Eviscerator, are you not?"

Vex doesn't answer. The relentless pang of the gut ghouls is inconceivable. Vex stands and stumbles to the kitchen, looking for the worm juice. Ana follows as Vex struggles to open the bottle. She grabs it and smashes it on the ground, eye glistening with hunger. Vex looks at her, disappointed. She thought she knew better.

They struggle for several moments, hand-to-hand, hard punches, hair pulling, bites and kicks. With force that felt superhuman, Vex flips Ana upside-down, smashing her against the kitchen floor. She breaks off one of Ana's metal talon rings and stabs her with it. She reaches her hand into Ana's stomach, takes several deep breaths, and rips out a mess of plastic tubes and writhing gut ghouls. Their translucent skin darkens by the second, exposed to the toxicity of oxygen. Ana's face turn purple as her look of shock fades to death-exhaustion. She reaches down, attempting to hold in her guts, but has lost all the strength in her hands. From neck to belly, her body became a great open wound. Tears stream down her cheeks. Vex can't look Ana in the eye. While one hand holds the necks of the gut ghouls, strangling them, the other reaches up to her face.

"He already knows." She whispers.

Ana dies with Vex's hand inside her. Within seconds, Ana's body disintegrates into grey dust.

Vex holds the corpses of the gut ghouls by the intestinal roots, examining them with hateful curiosity. They shrivel up and turn stone-grey in her hand. Opalescent tendrils float up through her nostrils and her eyes. Vex's ghostly pallor recedes, giving way to a healthy, pink hue in her skin, but only for a moment. Her breathing slows and her face seems to be more gaunt by the breath.

If we could see these other worlds, what would become of us? Surely not what had become of those purported to be great men. The artists, the philosophers, the fools afflicted by some deeper vision that cut through the static of everyday life. That shed a light onto the thick, amalgamated traffic of an unseen dimension. We can only suspect such things. But with art so prolific and wondrous, the question will always arise as to the conjurer. Were they master or witness? Portrayer or betrayer? Did they cast some unspoken light upon other worlds, nether worlds, after worlds? Were they told what was coming?

Von Aurovitch has been dead for over one hundred years, and yet his influence is pervasive. Ana hoped to never hear his name again, but she knew she would never escape it after that meeting. Like so many men of art whose hands drip with the black ink of cosmic indifference. The faces they paint will remain. The words they write will sing out forever. Somewhere. Someplace. Sometime. Spontanabre.

"Von Aurovitch was…" she began. Collins interrupted.

"Von Aurovitch, in his morbid isolation, found leisure

time enough to turn himself into his own diabolical divinity. Whether or not he reaped the benefits of those events, no one knows. "

"And you?"

He laughed.

"I know much more about the fate of Goethern Von Aurovitch than I care to discuss. I only wish you peace and safety on your journey home. Go back to the States. Tell them of me. Tell them I am old and frail. That my skills have given way to make room for immense paranoia and existential suffering."

"These are lies."

"Then tell them everything you wish to tell them. It will be of no consequence on my end. But do me one favor."

"What?"

"Keep me abreast of your research.

Ana froze, shocked at this assertion.

"Excuse me?"

"The Transpermia project. You were awarded the lead role in that experiment, were you not?"

She paused and looked at the grounds beyond their table. His energy was so faint, she toiled with the notion that he was an apparition. Some weary ghost tethered to a crumbling tower on the eve of earth's last quiet contemplation. Her mind shot back to the first Spontanabre victim she had encountered. They didn't let her see the dust. Only the vast white shroud covering it. The shroud, and the strange grey serpents pulled from the gut, turned to stone. This, she would remember.

IN URGENCY: VEX VALIS

This notice comes to you on the present day, 13 OCTOBER 2019 to notify you of the following: The EVISCERATOR demands your presence at 747 MATITY PLAZA in the BASEMENT FACILITY for AGGREGATE COUNCIL and MISSION ASSESMENT. Be advised that scheduled VISITATIONS are NON-NEGOTIABLE and absence will result in EXTRACTION CLAUSE 862: TORMENT AND DISMEMBERMENT.

Regards,

Q. T. MALIC
ORDER OF THE EVISCERAL SECRATERIUM

The façade is charred. The windows smashed. Vex passes through the opening that used to have a door, entering the ruins of the bakery with decided melancholy. An air of gloom soaks the place. All pink caked in black dust. Cakes themselves squashed, filled with shards of glass, impaled beetles, infection and fire.

Vex scans the room, looking for Colette. She doesn't call out. She's not that dumb. The door to the refrigerator room is ajar. Grabbing a jagged shard of glass from the shattered display case, she arms herself and walks slowly to the back.

The floor is soaked. A sickly smell of rotting food pervades the refrigerator, ice melting in every direction, sticky walls and shelves. The secret door to the subterranean chamber is already open, the stalactite snapped in half. Vex descends the staircase and stands before the entryway, astonished at the sight before her.

The clocks are gone.

The empty chasm screams the echoes of lost footsteps. A single pile of grey dust sits in the center of the chamber, blowing away in bursts as strange winds stir up from a lingering nothingness in motion. Vex kneels down next to the dust. It's all that's left of Colette.

She reaches into the center of the pile and pulls up a handful of long, white stones. The remnants of dead gut ghouls.

"No pain any more," she says. Colette could be at peace. She hopes she is, but there's a whole arena of dark thoughts dedicated to wondering what happens to the afflicted after death. Maybe there is nothing beyond the veil of life. Or maybe a special hell—- one of the Eviscerator's, more elaborate and tormenting than this living one. Unable to allow herself that level of thought, Vex pulls out moon dust and takes a hearty sniff. She stands, hands caked in grey dust, stomach screaming.

She woke up in agony. All was dark in the lab. As Valis groped around the floor, she found that she was in front of the northern wall, around thirty feet from the sheath. When she began working with the sheath, she was five-foot three and of average build. After her third entrance into the sheath, her height had increased to six feet. She had become so thin that on the way home, people stopped in disgust and concern: often the former and rarely the latter. But this wasn't the only transformation she would suffer. It wasn't the usual anemic pallor that set into her skin. Rather, it was a sickly greenish-brown that suggested bronze in a sewage plant. Her eyes caved in over deep, charcoal circles and her lips, though still full, cracked to the point of suggesting irreversible dehydration. The only part of her that remained healthy-looking was her teeth, which seemed to be stronger, whiter, and longer. Where once saw a stable, healthy women in the mirror, now was a gaunt, resurrected corpse. This was the power of the sheath. The power of the Eviscerator.

When one exists and thrives on a set of principles, their absolute eradication has merciless effects.

Merciless, because they now come to a position of nothing. No insight, no knowledge, no theory. When thrust into the cosmic unknown, the body and mind operate only on instinct. If that is a curse or a gift, Valis didn't know.

How often do we set time aside to think upon the unfamiliar? Very few engage in such enlightening practices, particularly in professions of joviality and routine. She was afforded difference. Her life's work was unfamiliarity put into practice. True, untouched experimentation is a privilege to be explored by a precious few. And to do so whilst remaining humble is perhaps an impossible feat. She wavered. Not only in thought but in rhythm. As the sheath progressed, she sensed it. Sensed that her comfort and esteem had been quantifiable. Not only by the protruding fungi on the western wall, but by some intangible force she sensed at all times. Growing weary, she began to embrace an innocence of manner whenever she mixed a new batch of Red. But it had all proven itself to be malevolent.

As Valis walked home, her mind was clouded by fragmentary, irrational thoughts.

The Eviscerator doesn't even have a star. He lives beside the pulse of the lavender incorporeality. 'Before she entered the apartment building, she vomited deep blue blood in the alleyway.

Her mood is far more ominous than usual. But she is quiet.

"What are you all serious about?"

He pulls up to the side street. He'd dropped her off in front of the warehouse nearly twenty times and still had no clue where she went when she turned the corner. She leans against the partition.

"I don't like this," he continues.

"Like what?"

Eric hesitates.

"The job."

Vex leans back. For a moment he thinks he feels fear in her, but that can't be it.

"You're quitting?"

"No... but I might need a week off, kid."

"No. " She is horrified.

"I can also quit outright."

"Please..."

He looks back at her. She's tearing up.

"I feel safe here."

"I know you do."

She reaches over to place her hand on his. He pulls

away. Eric laughs, trying to dispel the awkwardness. She is hurt by it.

"Listen, kid. You're gonna find yourself a great, rich guy. He'll have all the trappings and connections, you'll meet him at one of these industry parties. It might take a few hits, but you'll find one. And he'll have so much to offer. And you'll feel safe everywhere. Not just in a damn car."

"Fuck you! That's not what this is about."

Eric hesitates, embarrassed. He averts his eyes.

"Well, I don't know what anything is about. I just drive."

Why is it, do you think, that you are watched so intently from the sky? Why does the universe align so that you are constantly saved? It is not because that piece you carry is one of many. It is because it is one of the most essential of many. A storm within a storm. Such things are not for the faint of heart, of mind. Such things are not for young souls. Do not fear to be anonymous. Do not fear to be scolded, or doubted as to your strength. They are but marks during your passage through this place, onto the gilded mountain.

Aaron and Vex sat together in the living room in the light of one small candle. He sat in his chair while she sat on the floor. The length of her limbs caused immense discomfort. Her skin continued to peel. Vex fought irrational thoughts in an attempt to preserve her mind. She couldn't fathom the loss of her mental faculties. As much as she had denied herself the act of fulfilling Aaron's wish, she knew that beyond that night, the choice would no longer be hers. Thoughts led her to the possibility that she was experiencing a transient version of the affliction. The thought that Aaron had spent these past years trapped in those hellish places hardened her final resolve. She would free him of this evil once and for all. She owed him that, after all this time. Had he seen beyond the sheath, without its coaxing, or its company? The horrors she experienced were a temporary luxury compared to the limitless onset he had faced. All while she turned a blind eye.

Valis held the syringe in her hand. Their pact was sacrosanct, and she stalled in carrying out its final action. She could do so no longer. Aaron's battle with terminal confinement was her scarlet letter. She could not have lived behind that clouded window, but he had endured with silent agony and contemplation. Of what, she could only imagine. Valis held the syringe tightly. It took several minutes for her to the press the needle in. It was then that Aaron squeezed her hand. She looked at him. The fog in his eyes gave way to brightness for a quiet moment. That final grasp of clarity after years of torment was something she never deemed possible.

Baby girl, he thought. *I love her.*

As swiftly as that gift had broken through the barrier of their shared disease, it faded. He released her hand and passed on.

Vex wakes up onstage—piercing screams surrounding her, faces looming from every direction. The room spins violently—a remnant of sheath experience. She wonders if the voyages through the sheath were merely a serum-induced hallucination, but her mind is not in the proper state to question such things now. She fucked up. Blacked out during the show. Remembered too much.

She is afraid. More afraid than she had ever been. It was as though Aaron's death signaled some profound transition into worlds far above her. Whatever entities reside in such places were stirring. Her mind smothers her with ghastly narratives as she struggles to maintain her sanity. Why is she remembering it all now? She drags her body across the stage, blood and glitter sticking to her skin, and props herself up against the door. The Eviscerator. He's fucking with her. He really does know.

She stumbles backstage. In the darkness, she can see a shadow lurking in the far corner. Vex stands still in abject fear as the shadow approaches. It evaporates before reaching her, though the sensation of something passing through her body disturbs her senses. The gut ghouls squirm in satiated ecstasy.

Arthur, she thinks. *I have to check on Arthur.*

"Trespassing," She croaked, choking on spit. Her appearance startled Arthur.

"Vex…"

The twin fungi began breathing louder from the western wall. He turned to approach them. The moonlight fell on their phallic forms. Their teeth had grown several inches longer while she was away. Arthur looked at them with both horror and recognition. He let out several deep breaths, leaning against the lab bench. Vex felt like stones had been thrown at her chest. Every breath was excruciating. Arthur blinked calmly. She sensed that some resolve had set into him. He walked towards her.

"Magic seems so much more probable near the threshold, doesn't it?"

She snorted and winced at the same time. "I don't believe in magic."

"What is science, but magic calculated?"

"What the hell are you talking about?"

He reached out and peeled dead skin off of her forehead. Blue blood ran down her face.

"Vex, the sheath."

Panic set in. Valis coughed heavily and stumbled towards the counter. She took out the yellow serum and collapsed into his arms.

"Take this. In case you've been exposed. " Valis held out the vial. Yellow foam was beginning to gather around her teeth. She dropped the serum vial on the ground. It shattered.

The twin fungi hissed viciously from the western wall. She stood and unlocked the overhead cupboard, removing a hidden blade. The fungi turned their heavy heads, hissing at her on approach. She raised the blade and brought it down on the first with all of her strength. The other fungi screamed as the light blue blood of its twin splattered over Arthur. She raised the blade again, and brought it down upon the second. The skin on her back began to tingle. The sheath undulated with particular fury, screaming light and horrid sucking sounds. Before they knew what had happened, Arthur and Valis were both dragged into the sheath.

Very little could be seen beyond a yellow vortex of airborne liquid and flesh. The matter closed in fragments as silence broke into loud whirring. They both tried to scream, but no longer had mouths. With the sensation of every bone in their bodies cracking into dust...

He's gone. Wheelchair gone. S Book pages gone. But there isn't any dust, and that is as hopeful a sign as any. Vex examines every inch of Arthur's shithole apartment, looking for any trace of him, any clue to where he may be. Nothing. Her first thought is that the Eviscerator has taken him, but her instincts say otherwise.

She hopes he got out. That he found away. He was smart enough, not quite as sick, not deteriorating quite the same. There was resolve there. Arthur had always been the resilient one. Vex respected that. Maybe that's why she clung so tightly to him. He made her feel alive again, more than moon dust. But not as much as music. She walks over to his vintage radio and turns the dial. Siouxsie. Cities in Dust.

The pain did not cease in the lab. Vex looked down at her hands. They were three times their original size. The nails were sharper, and her skin, nearly translucent. Arthur struggled to stand. Given the new weight of their bodies, their knees buckled with each step towards the door. The sheath pulsed violently. Arthur screamed a scream impossible from the mouths of men, when he realized his legs were bloody stumps.

It is an ambition unto itself, to remain wholly quiet and at peace with the natural world. To be still in the throes of a chaos undefined. Vex opened the cupboard. Pulling bottle after bottle, she searched for the most flammable chemical in stock. She pulled it down and unscrewed the cap, approaching the sheath, soaking it with pungent muck and casting away the bottle. The moment came for one last look around the lab.

More things had happened here than convention stood to recount. Valis tried to recall every moment of significance to bring some meaning to the end, but as so often happens when attempting to summon nostalgia, all that she remembered had become malignantly flat. Indifferent. Meaningless. She lit the match. The sheath rippled violently in the inferno.

It may very well have been some fortune... the sickness

that blinded her to the embers. All the world turned grey and she could hear but the swallows of innocent parties and the crackling of steps near and far. She would not be a contender in the race of intellect any longer. She cringed at her former blindness in thinking that greatness would save her. The spirit does not digest blame as it does ignorance. The microbes were undoubtedly a cosmic seed, allowing them passage through to this unseen world. If dark things can be so fiercely encouraged, very little else haunts the mind. Valis questioned her own capacity for such wonder, as all do when sanctuary collapses and one escapes the wreckage by the skin of their teeth. If she and Arthur were in the company of ancients, they were having one hell of a laugh.

"You've obeyed the summons."

The Eviscerator, in that foetid splendor, pulls intestines from a gaping ram. Worms are stuffed into its nostrils... a clear spy of the Worm King. He looks down at the gut hovel with a face obscured by his deep yellow and metal-plated mask and decapitates the beast. Unusually hunched and spreading the creature's skin back with his knotted fingers, he leans his arm, opal-clad and languid, on the twisting horns of the lifeless animal.

Do you like the smell, Vex Valis?

He speaks to her in cerebral tongues, but never in front of living animals. He thinks it disrespectful. The Eviscerator invades her mind with fervor, making her itch. She blows a puff of green smoke towards the back of his head, sucking on a black cigarette.

"I know who the Conspirator is."

The Eviscerator stops, dropping the organs back onto the table. He turns his head only, pure white eyes bearing down into her.

Oh?

She drops her cigarette to the concrete grime, twisting it under her signature boot. Walking over to the table, she dips her finger in the corpse of the ram. The Eviscerator, containing the urge to speak, watches her press her finger to the bricks on the northern wall, swiping the blood in a calligraphic odyssey he had long desired to watch.

That. Is. It.

She has written her own name on the wall.

"Vex Valis, you are very sick."

"Sick! I am sick. But I will not tell you where I keep my armies. " For all splintered and splattered under the weight of her delicate hands. Wondrous horrors and the cruelties of monsters are most effective in the hands of brutalized women. And sweet poison is sweetest after hours of bleeding and dreaming and living.

I cannot eat, but breathe

Turning towards him, she drops her dress, revealing her mangled naked form. The scar remains from her evisceration, but the tell-tale signs of gut-ghoul inhabitation are absent. As the last mangled thread of her dress hits the ground, the worms in the rafters above tip over their buckets. Wormjuice rains down over them, soaking the Eviscerator.

I cannot drink, but dry up.

Time freezes as the liquid soaks into his flesh, an inconceivable matter to begin with. Magnetic forces pull Vex toward him. They collide, the Eviscerator emitting alien screams that lure her into momentary deafness. Vex struggles to be free of him, landing brutal punches to its neck and face, injuring herself on the metal obscuring his features. She grows weaker. As his flesh begins to melt, she pries the mask from him. The great gaping maw—a mouth of sorts—is a void of darkness almost impossible to look at. She closes her eyes and vomits the last drops of wormjuice into the mouth of the Eviscerator. It doesn't kill him. Radiation builds. Her skin is turning yellow. As she wavers in and out of consciousness, losing her grip, Melville crawls out from her bra and enters the mouth of the Eviscerator. A few moments pass. He chews his way out of his chest, dragging up the remnants of a black heart, bleeding gasoline blood. The beetle shrivels, soaked in the horror of death. Vex stands away from the twin corpses and runs for the door as the Eviscerator begins to evaporate. Unknown spectrums of light force her into shock-delirium. Endless halls grow longer, floors undulate like disturbed oceans. She reaches the main door of the warehouse and rushes out onto the street.

I cannot love, but lie alone in hunger.

Quiet snow. Eric wants to find peace in the falling, like he did when he was younger, but some things you can only see through dead eyes. Vex comes to life in it. She finds joy in the simplest things. He keeps quiet and watches her savor small moments of life. It's only been a week since he quit. He misses her.

It only takes a few days for the full brunt of unemployment to hit. The kids are going back to school, and Eric can barely make what he needs to get them fed. All he needed to do was keep his mouth shut, keep a distance, and do the job. But those old instincts kicked in.

What haunts Eric nightly is nothing more than a whistle in far away sands. He drowns away the sound in various glasses. He could speak to those lonely moments when one becomes aware of their true surroundings, but he tries to abstain from the torments of the sentimental in his waking hours.

The car was one of the nicest parts of the job. She paid for the trade-in. A luxury sedan. Black, comfortable. Way out of his range, but she foot the bill, which he appreciated. Vex made sure he logged mileage too so she could cover the gas. God knows she could afford it.

The car disappeared a few nights after the last time he drove her. He had no clue who could have stolen it, but knew they must have been pretty damn proficient, to break the door code. That's what he tells himself. He reported it missing, but hasn't heard anything about it since.

Two in the morning, a few weeks later, Eric hears the engine in front of the apartment building. He throws on a t-shirt and runs outside.

He can see her. Arms dangling outside the window, bangles and all, holding onto a cigarette.

"Vex, what the fuck? What is…"

In the passenger seat beside her is the carcass of a man, or monster? Burned and brutalized beyond recognition. It reeks, like oysters and stale cum.

"I need your help, Eric."

"Get out of the car."

She barely blinks an eye as she takes a puff of her cigarette. Eric is furious.

"Get out of the fucking car!"

She stares at him, throwing the cigarette out onto the pavement. Vex slowly emerges, limping severely. He's never seen her that ill. A mere apparition of the girl he knew.

"Vex. . . what is this?"

"Will you help me or not?"

He searches her face, looking for a reason. She won't look at him.

"Who is he?" I asked her.

"Who the fuck do you think?"

"The Eviscerator?"

Vex looks into his eyes, fear-soaked and waiting.

Eric turns around, pacing for a few moments with his hand over his mouth.

"Why didn't you leave him, wherever?"

"They would have found him."

"Oh, and they won't find him here?"

She drops her cigarette and puts it out with her stiletto.

"Not if you help me dump him. I can't lift him myself."

Vex points to the back seat of the car. Eric moves around her and sticks his head in the open window. Ana Cristalen, also dead. Eric turns around in shock, searching Vex's eyes for something to comfort him, but there is nothing.

"Kid…"

She pushes him up against the car.

"Kid? Does this look like something a fucking kid is capable of? Well?"

She pushes him again.

"Does it?"

Eric grabs her wrists gently to prevent her from hitting him. She struggles for a moment, and then breaks down. He holds onto her as she leans into his chest.

"Ok, Vex. Get in the car."

They dump the Eviscerator's body first. It takes a while to sink, but eventually makes its way down to the black depths of the water beneath the dock. Ana Cristalen sinks much slower.

Eric gets back into the car. Vex slides into the passenger seat. The smell of burnt flesh remains. Eric lets the windows down, hoping a bit of the sea air will clear it out. It doesn't.

He can't look at her. She stares at him. Out of the corner of his eye, he sees her remove her shirt, revealing open wounds in her stomach. They gush blood, pus, tubes, translucent fog. Pale grey dust forms around the wound, flaking off with increasing speed. She isn't hungry anymore. Eric's eyes ask the question his mouth can't bear to.

"A few minutes," she says

He looks away, trying to make sense of what Vex is telling him.

"What was I to you this whole time, Vex? Collateral damage?"

"No."

Tears fill her eyes. She climbs over the seat and sits on top of him. She places both hands on his face, kisses him, presses her forehead against his and holds it there. She closes her eyes and breathes.

"You just drive."

Farah Rose Smith is a poet, fiction writer, musician, and artist from Providence, Rhode Island. She is the founder and editor of Mantid Magazine, which publishes weird fiction from diverse women, and the creative director of Grimoire Pictures, a microscopic film company. Her work, which often focuses on the Surreal and Avant-garde, has been recognized at film festivals, receiving accolades in screenwriting and experimental film.

F4
Larissa Glasser

A cruise ship on the back of a sleeping kaiju. A transgender bartender trying to come terms with who she is. A rift in dimensions known as The Sway. A cruel captain. A storm of turmoil, insanity and magic is coming together and taking the ship deep into the unknown. What will Carol the bartender learn in this maddening non-place that changes bodies and minds alike into bizarre terrors? What is the sleeping monster who holds up the ship trying to tell her? What do Carol's fractured sense of self and a community of internet trolls have to do with the sudden pull of The Sway?

Polymer
Caleb Wilson

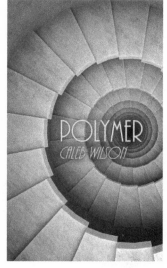

You've seen monster hunts before. You've watched as a guy with throwing axes and ninja stars ascends stairs to fight a big furry werewolf with tentacles or a floating head of indeterminate origin. You've seen hunters. But you've never seen Polymer. Polymer's got style, Polymer's got sex appeal, Polymer's got panache. And you, lucky reader, get to join us right behind the glass in Sickleburg Castle where the battle of the century is about to commence. Who is the man behind the music, the monsters, the guts, the gore and the glory? Get ready for an event like no other.

Winnie
Katy Michelle Quinn

Winnie and Colt forever. Winnie is Colt's one and only, Colt is Winnie's true love. Winnie is Colt's rifle. There is nothing Winnie wants more than to please Colt and since a rifle is everything the young cowboy's ever wanted, she certainly does that. But one day Winnie finds that she is not a rifle but in fact a woman. Can Winnie keep the sparks between them ignited, even if she isn't the gun of his dreams. What happens if she can't?

Eviscerator
Farah Rose Smith

Vex Valis—doctor. Vex Valis—rocker. Vex Valis—iconoclast. You would think Vex Valis has it all but what Vex has is a secret that rots away at her from her very core. Vex is infected with Gut Ghouls and will do anything to be rid of them, even if it means consorting with subterranean worms or blending science and the occult in dangerous and unsavory ways. You may envy Vex's jet setting Dark Wave scientist lifestyle but you won't when you see the trials incurred when she catches the attention of a being that rends people and worlds alike, the scrutiny of…The Eviscerator

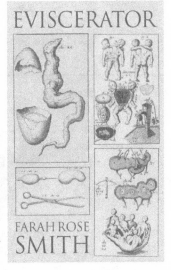

Fell Beauties
Leigham Shardlow

In the last outpost of ugliness in the world, beautiful people are falling from the sky. When Fat Janet is kicked out of the buffet where she has holed up for food and safety, she is forced to confront not only the reality of perfect falling bodies but the attentions of an overzealous plastic surgeon and his followers. She teams up with a mystery man in hopes of getting out of this alive but soon finds that confronting the problem head on is the only option. Can imperfection survive this beautiful disaster?

Crime of the Scene
Shawn Koch

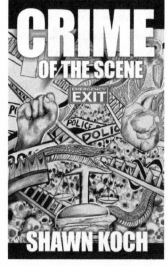

A detective investigating a crime scene finds that nested inside this crime scene is another, and inside that another. Demons, physical deformity, body switching and endless trials await him as he begins to face his own transgressions. Reality grows distant as he soon comes to realize that he has stumbled not only upon the scene of many crimes but of all crimes. He might just have what it takes to get to the bottom of these but only if he gets to the bottom of himself.

CPSIA information can be obtained
at www.ICGtesting.com
Printed in the USA
LVHW040901150622
721313LV00003B/530